BECOMING JANE

BECOMING JANE

The Wit and Wisdom of Jane Austen

Edited by Anne Newgarden

miramax books

HYPERION

NEW YORK

Copyright © 2007 Hyperion

Library of Congress Cataloging-in-Publication Data

Austen, Jane, 1775–1817.
    Becoming Jane : the wit and wisdom of Jane Austen / edited by
Anne Newgarden.—1st ed.
        p. cm.
    ISBN-13: 978-1-4013-0904-6
    ISBN-10: 1-4013-0904-6
    1. Austen, Jane, 1775–1817—Quotations.   2. Austen, Jane,
1775–1817—Humor.   3. Wisdom in literature.   I. Newgarden, Anne.
II. Title.
    PR4032.N49 2007
    823'.7—dc22   2007061310

Hyperion books are available for special promotions, premiums, and corporate training. For details contact Michael Rentas, Proprietary Markets, Hyperion, 77 West 66th Street, 12th floor, New York, New York 10023, or call 212-456-0133.

Book Design by Helene Berinsky

FIRST EDITION

1   3   5   7   9   10   8   6   4   2

To my father, for teaching me to love books.
And to my mother, for everything.

CONTENTS

PREFACE

It is a truth universally acknowledged that Jane Austen, the clergyman's daughter from Hampshire, England, who quietly penned six masterpieces more than two centuries ago, is more popular today than ever.

Austen's books, still eagerly devoured by readers of all ages, have inspired fictional spin-offs of every stripe, from a legion of *Pride and Prejudice* sequels, to a mystery series starring the authoress herself as sleuth, to a contemporary tale about a quirky reading group dedicated solely to her works. What's more, Austen's novels have been translated into just about every storytelling medium imaginable—movies, miniseries, graphic novels, stage plays and musicals, operettas, and ballets. There's a

Jane Austen dating guide, a Jane Austen cookbook, and even a Jane Austen action figure, complete with ruffled mobcap and removable writing quill.

But *why* this Jane mania? What is it that makes us continually crave the unique sense and sensibility that is Jane?

The answer, of course, lies in her work. Austen, who lived a brief forty-one years (not even long enough to see her last two novels published), never traveled beyond her native England, and led what many regard as an "unremarkable" life, has long been acknowledged as one of our greatest writers. Her elegant prose, biting wit, and keen insights on the workings of the human heart and the follies and frailties of human nature have garnered her a vast and diverse fan club. Beyond this, though, her work, while firmly of its time in its depiction of societal constraints and mores, transcends the boundaries of "period" fiction by brilliantly capturing truth after unchanging truth about human behavior, experience, and emotion.

Austen's men and women—ball gowns, bonnets, and breeches aside—are not so very different from men and women today. While obviously they face completely different obstacles in their pursuit of marital happiness, Austen's favorite subject, their feelings and failings, their vices and vulnerabilities provoke in modern-day readers (or viewers, as the case may be) a nod of recognition. "All the privilege I claim for my own sex," says Anne Elliot in *Persuasion,* ". . . is that of loving longest, when existence or when hope is gone." Could this sentiment feel fresher if it were written yesterday? Or this, from *Northanger Abbey*: "Friendship is certainly the finest balm for the pangs of disappointed love." Or how about this one, from Henry Crawford in *Mansfield Park:* "I cannot be satisfied without Fanny Price, without making a small hole in Fanny Price's heart."

As these quotes, like many of those that fill this volume, show, Austen was a master of human observation. It's the life blood of her books, and her personal correspondence, too. And what do we human creatures love more than to hold up a mirror to ourselves? Reveling in the first blush of love, or mourning its loss—remembering who we once were, or impatient for who we hope to become—we turn to our own reflection for knowledge, for solace, for pity, for hope, or for the sheer pleasure it gives us. It's no wonder we keep coming back to Jane Austen, over and over again. Among her treasure trove of writerly gifts, two, for me, stand out.

She had an uncanny ability to *get* people, and a genius for transmitting her laser-sharp perceptions of them onto the page, sometimes with one masterful stroke (which is where the power of her wit often lies), but often layer by complex layer, as her characters slowly grow in self-knowledge or in their understanding of one another—usually both. And isn't that, when it comes down to it, what we're all after (or at least, those of us who have sought out more than a passing acquaintance with Jane)?

"Wisdom is better than Wit, & in the long run will certainly have the laugh on her side," Austen wrote in a letter to her niece Fanny Knight. Though far be it from me to call Jane Austen a moralist, her writing does have an element of the instructive. Her leading ladies (and gentlemen) grow and change for the better, and the rest of her characters, in most cases, anyway, get the endings they deserve. So I think that she would be pleased with the far-reaching scope of her multimedia legacy, pleased to continue to pass on her particular brand of wisdom (and wit, too, of course) to more and more of us who both need it and delight in it—or, at least, the ones who deserve it.

I hope that the reading of these excerpts will bring as much pleasure as did their gathering. I have tried as much as possible, especially in her letters, to preserve Austen's original, and often quite unique, spelling and punctuation. Whether this is your first exposure to Austen or your fiftieth, I hope that these quotes will inspire you to crack open her books, seek out the adaptations, and more deeply experience her magic.

FAMILY

Family—with all its blessings, comforts, torments, and absurdities—plays a pivotal role in the lives of all of Jane Austen's characters, as her own family did in hers. Austen was born on December 16, 1775, into a large and tight-knit family—the seventh of eight children: six boys and two girls. Although her second eldest brother, George, who suffered from seizures and perhaps also deafness and other disorders, was not raised at Steventon with the rest, several cousins made extended visits at various times and, with the addition of the student boarders that her parents took in, the seven-bedroom house in which Jane grew up was a lively and bustling place. It is described by those who visited her family as being filled with witty and thought-provoking conversation, a large library of well-read books, and the frequent performances of home theatricals (much like those Austen wrote about in *Mansfield Park*), particularly those of the satirical, comedy-of-manners sort. Jane, who as an adolescent began writing her own plays, poems, and literary parodies to amuse her family (and no doubt herself), certainly thrived creatively in this rich and stimulating environment, embarking on a serious literary career by the age of twenty, when she began *First Impressions* (later revised into *Pride and Prejudice*).

Austen was close, to varying degrees, to the brothers with whom she was raised. James, the eldest, also had literary leanings; he wrote poetry and, while he was at Oxford, he started a periodical for gentlemen called *The Loiterer,* which he edited with their brother Henry. Later he became a clergyman, taking over the duties at Steventon after his father retired. Edward, the third, was adopted in his teens by wealthy, childless cousins of the Austens, who were seeking an heir, and were extraordinarily fond of him. (He later officially took on their surname, Knight.) Henry, born fourth, who is said to have been Jane's favorite and who was witty and less serious than his brothers, handled many of the details of publishing her work. He married his first cousin, the glamorous Eliza de Feuillide, whose first husband, a French count, had been guillotined, and who was ten years Henry's senior. Later in life Henry, like James, became a clergyman. Frank (Francis) and Charles, the two youngest boys, entered the navy at an early age, and were away at sea much of the time (though their influence is apparent in the many naval references that appear in *Mansfield Park* and *Persuasion*). Both eventually rose to the rank of admiral.

Jane was by far the closest to her only sister, Cassandra, nearly three years her senior. Neither of the sisters ever wed. The two shared a home and, in fact, a bedroom, for the whole of their lives, with Cassandra and her mother (up until her death) carrying out most of the domestic duties. This arrangement lasted until July 18, 1817, when Jane passed away with her head in her sister's lap. Their lifelong intimacy is clear in the frequency of the newsy, chatty letters exchanged between the two whenever they were apart. Jane strove to amuse Cassandra, as she often pointed out in the letters, and her arch, often outrageous observations and insults about their mutual friends and acquaintances were obviously spurred on by that desire.

Austen also had a very large extended family, and frequently traveled to visit them. She felt great affection especially toward the profusion of nephews and nieces provided by her brothers; she seemed to have a special affinity for the role of aunt, and often wrote to her nieces Fanny Knight (later Knatchbull), Anna Austen (later Lefroy), and Caroline Austen; and to her nephew James Edward Austen (later Austen-Leigh, having added a second surname when he became his aunt's— Mrs. Leigh Perrot's—heir). They sought her advice, both of the romantic and the literary sort, as writing talent seemed to run thickly in the Austen blood (Jane's mother, though lacking a great deal of formal education, was known to be a clever letter writer, and also quite adept at rhyming verse), and three of these four nieces and nephews published memoirs revealing a great deal of affection for their Aunt Jane.

"It is very unfair to judge of anybody's conduct, without an intimate knowledge of their situation. Nobody, who has not been in the interior of a family, can say what the difficulties of any individual of that family may be."

—*Emma Woodhouse to Mr. Knightley, in* Emma

* * *

A family of ten children will always be called a fine family, where there are heads and arms and legs enough for the number; but the Morlands had little other right to the word, for they were in general very plain . . .

—*from* Northanger Abbey

* * *

I am greatly pleased with your account of Fanny; I found her in the summer just what you describe, almost another Sister, & could not have supposed that a neice would ever have been so much to me. She is quite after one's own heart.

—*from a letter to her sister, Cassandra, about their niece Fanny Knight, October 7–9, 1808*

* * *

Miss Frances married, in the common phrase, to disoblige her family, and by fixing on a Lieutenant of Marines, without education, fortune, or connections, did it very thoroughly.

—*from* Mansfield Park

* * *

You will have a great deal of unreserved discourse with Mrs K. [Mrs. Knight, their brother Edward's adoptive mother], I dare say, upon this subject, as well as upon many other of our family matters. Abuse everybody but me.

—*from a letter to her sister, Cassandra, January 7–8,* 1807

* * *

My dear itty Dordy's [Edward Austen (Knight)'s second son, George, Jane's nephew] remembrance of me is very pleasing to me; foolishly pleasing, because I know it will be over so soon. My attachment to him will be more durable; I shall think with tenderness & delight on his beautiful & smiling Countenance & interesting Manners, till a few years have turned him into an ungovernable, ungracious fellow.

—*from a letter to her sister, Cassandra, October 27–28, 1798*

* * *

This . . . brought them to the door of Mrs. Thorpe's lodgings. . . . "Ah, mother! how do you do?" said he, giving her a hearty shake of the hand: "Where did you get that quiz of a hat? it makes you look like an old witch. Here is Morland and I come to stay a few days with you, so you must look out for a couple of beds somewhere near." And this address seemed to satisfy all the fondest wishes of the mother's heart, for she received him with the most delighted and exulting affection. On his two younger sisters he then bestowed an equal portion of his fraternal tenderness, for he asked each of them how they did, and observed that they both looked very ugly.

—*on John Thorpe, in* Northanger Abbey

* * *

To Elizabeth it appeared, that had her family made an agreement to expose themselves as much as they could during the evening, it would have been impossible for them to play their parts with more spirit, or finer success; and happy did she think it for Bingley and her sister that some of the exhibition had escaped his notice, and that his feelings were not of a sort to be much distressed by the folly which he must have witnessed.

—*on Elizabeth Bennet, in* Pride and Prejudice

* * *

His having been in love with the Aunt, gives Cecilia an additional Interest with him. I like the Idea;—a very proper compliment to an Aunt!—I rather imagine indeed that Neices are seldom chosen but in compliment to some Aunt or other. I dare say Ben [Anna's husband] was in love with me once, & w^d never have thought of *You* if he had not supposed me dead of a Scarlet fever.

—*from a letter to her niece Anna (Austen) Lefroy, referring to characters in a novel that Anna was writing, which she sent to her Aunt Jane for her opinion, November* 30, 1814

* * *

. . . a fond mother, though, in pursuit of praise for her children, the most rapacious of human beings, is likewise the most credulous; her demands are exorbitant; but she will swallow anything.

—*on* Lady Middleton, *in* Sense and Sensibility

* * *

. . . Fanny had never known so much felicity in her life, as in this unchecked, equal fearless intercourse with the brother and friend . . . with whom . . . all the evil and good of their earliest years could be gone over again, and every former united pain and pleasure retraced with the fondest recollection. An advantage this, a strengthener of love, in which even the conjugal tie is beneath the fraternal. Children of the same family, the same blood, with the same first associations and habits, have some means of enjoyment in their power, which no subsequent connections can supply.

—*on* Fanny Price and her brother William, *in*
Mansfield Park

* * *

I give you joy of our new nephew, & hope if he ever comes to be hanged, it will not be till we are too old to care about it.

—*from a letter to her sister, Cassandra, April 25, 1811*
    (on the birth of their brother Francis William's second son)

* * *

You are inimitable, irresistable. You are the delight of my Life. . . . You are worth your weight in Gold, or even in the new Silver Coinage. . . . You are the Paragon of all that is Silly & Sensible, common-place & eccentric, Sad & Lively, Provoking & Interesting. . . . Oh! what a loss it will be, when you are married. You are too agreable in your single state, too agreable as a Neice.

—*from a letter to her niece Fanny Knight,*
    February 20–21, 1817

* * *

. . . I leave it to be settled by whomsoever it may concern, whether the tendency of this work be altogether to
recommend parental tyranny, or reward filial disobedi-
ence.

> —*from* Northanger Abbey, *referring to the fact that*
> *General Tilney's disapproval of Catherine Morland likely*
> *was conducive to his son's marrying her*

* * *

A lady, without a family, was the very best preserver of
furniture in the world.

> —*Mr. Shepherd's view, regarding potential tenants to lease*
> *Sir Walter Eliot's house, in* Persuasion

* * *

"There are secrets in all families . . ."

> —*Mr. Weston to Emma, in* Emma

* * *

JUVENILIA

*J*ane Austen's large and truly astonishing collection of early writings, referred to as her juvenilia, has only recently begun to get the kind of public attention that her six completed novels have long received—and that it deserves. Many of these works—sketches, short fiction, verse, several pieces of nonfiction, and the beginnings of some full-length novels—were written by Austen during her adolescent and teenage years (some, scholars think, as early as the age of twelve). Austen copied them into three notebooks that she titled *Volume the First*, *Volume the Second*, and *Volume the Third*, with her typical mock pomp and circumstance. Apparently written for the amusement of her family, to whom she would often read them aloud, they contain lavish dedications that are frequently as entertaining as the pieces themselves. Often satirizing the popular literary modes of her day (as she later did so memorably in *Northanger Abbey*), as well as social conventions and manners, these pieces practically jump off the page with their bold, sometimes absurdist humor, their remarkable sophistication, and their galloping exuberance. They also stand as an accurate preview of Austen's more mature work, revealing many of the themes that were to continue to engage her, including home life, courtship and marriage, and of course, human folly and frailty.

(Dates for the works have been omitted here, as many are difficult if not impossible to pin down. Also, as is usually the case with her juvenilia, Austen's original spellings have been left intact.)

To Miss Cooper

Cousin

Conscious of the Charming Character which in every Country, & every Clime in Christendom is Cried,

Concerning you, with Caution & Care I Commend to your Charitable Criticism this Clever Collection of Curious Comments, which have been Carefully Culled, Collected & Classed by your Comical Cousin

The Author

—*dedication of* A Collection of Letters, *to her cousin*
Jane Cooper

* * *

Sophia shreiked and fainted on the Ground—I screamed and instantly ran mad.—We remained thus mutually deprived of our Senses some minutes, and on regaining them were deprived of them again. For an Hour and a Quarter did we continue in this unfortunate Situation . . .

—*from* Love and Freindship: A novel in a series of Letters, *dedicated to "Madame la Comtesse de Feuillide,"*
Jane's cousin, who later married her brother Henry

* * *

. . . but e'er they had been many minutes seated, the Wit & Charms which shone resplendent in the conversation of the amiable Rebecca enchanted them so much that they all with one accord jumped up and exclaimed:

"Lovely & too charming Fair one, notwithstanding your forbidding Squint, your greasy tresses & your swelling Back, which are more frightfull than imagination can paint or pen describe, I cannot refrain from expressing my raptures, at the engaging Qualities of your Mind, which so amply atone for the Horror, with which your first appearance must ever inspire the unwary visitor.

"Your sentiments so nobly expressed on the different excellencies of Indian & English Muslins, & the judicious preference you give the former, have excited in me an admiration of which I can alone give an adequate idea, by assuring you it is nearly equal to what I feel for myself."

Then making a profound Curtesy to the amiable & abashed Rebecca, they left the room & hurried home.

—*from* Frederic and Elfrida: A Novel, *dedicated to Martha Lloyd (then Austen's neighbor, and later the second wife of her brother Francis), in thanks for her generosity in "finishing [Austen's] muslin Cloak"*

* * *

Henry the 4th ascended the throne of England much to his own satisfaction in the year 1399, after having prevailed on his cousin & predecessor Richard the 2d to resign it to him, & to retire for the rest of his Life to Pomfret Castle, where he happened to be murdered . . .

 —*from* The History of England, from the reign of
  Henry the 4th to the death of Charles the 1st,
  By a partial, prejudiced, & ignorant Historian.,
  dedicated to "Miss Austen," her sister, Cassandra

* * *

The Johnsons were a family of Love, & though a little addicted to the Bottle & the Dice, had many good Qualities.

 —*from* Jack and Alice: A Novel, *inscribed to her brother*
  "Francis William Austen Esq., Midshipman on board his
  Majesty's Ship the Perseverance, by his obedient humble
  Servant The Author"

* * *

Chapter the First

Cassandra was the Daughter & the only Daughter of a celebrated Millener in Bond Street. Her father was of noble Birth, being the near relation of the Dutchess of ———'s Butler.

Chapter the 2d

When Cassandra had attained her 16th year, she was lovely & amiable, & chancing to fall in love with an elegant Bonnet her Mother had just compleated, bespoke by the Countess of ———, she placed it on her gentle Head & walked from her Mother's shop to make her Fortune.

Chapter the 3d

The first person she met, was the Viscount of ———, a young Man, no less celebrated for his Accomplishments & Virtues, than for his Elegance & Beauty. She curtseyed & walked on.

Chapter the 4th

She then proceeded to a Pastry-cook's, where she devoured six ices, refused to pay for them, knocked down the Pastry Cook & walked away.

—*from* The Beautifull Cassandra: A Novel in Twelve Chapters, *dedicated to "Miss Austen," her sister, Cassandra*

* * *

For three months did the Masquerade afford ample subject for conversation to the inhabitants of Pammydiddle; but no character at it was so fully expatiated on as Charles Adams. The singularity of his appearance, the beams which darted from his eyes, the brightness of his Wit, & the whole *tout ensemble* of his person had subdued the hearts of so many of the young Ladies, that of the six present at the Masquerade but five had returned uncaptivated. Alice Johnson was the unhappy sixth whose heart had not been able to withstand the power of his Charms.

—*from* Jack and Alice: A Novel, *inscribed to her brother "Francis William Austen Esq., Midshipman on board his*

Majesty's Ship the Perseverance by his obedient humble Servant The Author"

* * *

Scene the 2d
The Dining Parlour.
Miss Fitzgerald *at top.* Lord Fitzgerald *at bottom. Company ranged on each side. Servants waiting.*

CLOE. I shall trouble Mr. Stanly for a Little of the fried Cow heel & Onion.

STANLY. Oh Madam, there is a secret pleasure in helping so amiable a Lady.—

LADY H. I assure you, my Lord, Sir Arthur never touches wine; but Sophy will toss off a bumper I am sure, to oblige your Lordship.

LORD F. Elder wine or Mead, Miss Hampton?

SOPHY. If it is equal to you, Sir, I should prefer some warm ale with a toast and nutmeg.

LORD F. Two glasses of warmed ale with a toast and nutmeg.

Miss F. I am afraid, Mr. Willoughby, you take no care of yourself. I fear you don't meet with any thing to your liking.

WILLOUGHBY. Oh! Madam, I can want for nothing while there are red herrings on table.

Lord F. Sir Arthur, taste that Tripe. I think you will not find it amiss.

Lady H. Sir Arthur never eats Tripe; tis too savoury for him, you know, my Lord.

Miss F. Take away the Liver & Crow, & bring in the suet pudding.

(a short Pause.)

Miss F. Sir Arthur, shan't I send you a bit of pudding?

Lady H. Sir Arthur never eats suet pudding, Ma'am. It is too high a Dish for him.

—*from* The Visit: A Comedy in Two Acts, *dedicated to "the Revd. James Austen," her brother*

* * *

This Monarch [Edward the 4th] was famous only for his Beauty & his Courage, of which the Picture we have here

given of him, & his undaunted Behaviour in marrying
one Woman while he was engaged to another, are sufficient proofs. . . . One of Edward's Mistresses was Jane
Shore, who has had a play written about her, but it is a
tragedy & therefore not worth reading.

> —*from* The History of England, from the reign of
> Henry the 4th to the death of Charles the 1st,
> By a partial, prejudiced, & ignorant Historian.,
> *dedicated to "Miss Austen," her sister, Cassandra*

*   *   *

I have a thousand excuses to beg for having so long de-
layed thanking you, my dear Peggy, for your agreable
Letter, which beleive me I should not have deferred
doing, had not every moment of my time during the
last five weeks been so fully employed in the necessary
arrangements for my sister's Wedding, as to allow me
no time to devote either to you or myself. And now
what provokes me more than anything else is that the
Match is broke off, and all my Labour thrown away.
Imagine how great the Dissapointment must be to

me, when you consider that after having laboured both by Night and Day, in order to get the Wedding dinner ready by the time appointed, after having roasted Beef, Broiled Mutton, and Stewed Soup enough to last the new-married Couple through the Honey-moon, I had the mortification of finding that I had been Roasting, Broiling and Stewing both the Meat and Myself to no purpose. Indeed my dear Freind, I never remember suffering any vexation equal to what I experienced on last Monday when my Sister came running to me in the Store-room with her face as White as a Whipt syllabub, and told me that Hervey had been thrown from his Horse, had fractured his Scull and was pronounced by his Surgeon to be in the most emminent Danger. "Good God!" (said I) "you don't say so? Why what in the name of Heaven will become of all the Victuals? . . ."

—*from* Lesley Castle: An unfinished Novel in Letters,
    dedicated to "Henry Thomas Austen Esqre.," her brother

*   *   *

This Young Lady, whose merits deserved a better fate than she met with, was the darling of her relations—From the clearness of her skin & the Brilliancy of her Eyes, she was fully entitled to all their partial affection. Another circumstance contributed to the general Love they bore her, and that was one of the finest heads of hair in the world.

　　—from Evelyn, *dedicated to "Miss Mary Lloyd"*
　　(who later became the second wife of Jane's eldest
　　brother, James)

* * *

MY DEAR NEICE

As I am prevented by the great distance between Rowling and Steventon from superintending Your Education Myself, the care of which will probably on that account devolve on your Father & Mother, I think it my particular Duty to prevent your feeling as much as possible the want of my personal instructions, by addressing to You on paper my Opinions & Admonitions on the conduct of Young Women, which you will find expressed in the following pages.—

I am my dear Neice

Your affectionate Aunt

The Author.

—*one of five pieces, now referred to as "Scraps," written to her*
newborn niece "Miss Fanny Catherine Austen" (later
Knight)

* * *

"Talk not to me of Phaetons (said I, raving in a frantic, in-
coherent manner)—Give me a violin.—I'll play to him
and sooth him in his melancholy Hours—Beware ye gentle Nymphs of Cupid's Thunderbolts, avoid the piercing
Shafts of Jupiter—Look at that Grove of Firs—I see a Leg
of Mutton—They told me Edward was not Dead; but they
deceived me—they took him for a Cucumber—" Thus I
continued wildly exclaiming on my Edward's Death.

—*from* Love and Freindship: A novel in a series of
Letters, *dedicated to "Madame la Comtesse de Feuillide,"*
Jane's cousin, who later married her brother Henry

* * *

"How could I be so forgetful as to sit down out of doors at such a time of night! I shall certainly have a return of my rheumatism after it—I begin to feel very chill already. I must have caught a dreadful cold by this time—I am sure of being lain-up all the winter after it—" Then reckoning with her fingers, "Let me see; This is July; the cold weather will soon be coming in—August—September—October—November—December—January—February—March—April—Very likely I may not be tolerable again before May. . . ."

—*from* Catharine, or the Bower, *dedicated to "Miss Austen," her sister, Cassandra*

* * *

We read, we work, we walk and when fatigued with these Employments relieve our spirits, either by a lively song, a graceful Dance, or by some smart bon-mot, and witty repartée. We are handsome, my dear Charlotte, very handsome and the greatest of our Perfections is, that we are entirely insensible of them ourselves.

—*from* Lesley Castle: An unfinished Novel in Letters,
    dedicated to "Henry Thomas Austen Esqre.," her brother

* * *

BEAUTY AND FASHION

In Jane Austen's world, as in the worlds of her novels, attending parties, balls, and teas was part of the regular course of events. Such affairs provided men and women with a way to mingle socially with their peers for lighthearted amusements such as dancing and playing cards, but also for the deadly serious business of seeking out eligible mates. With that in mind, dressing to impress was important. While Austen once wrote that men took little notice of women's attire, her letters reveal that she did make certain efforts with her own dress and hair (the latter of which seems to have given her no end of trouble). The color and cut of a gown, the fineness of its silk or muslin, and the choice of "sprig" atop a bonnet (flowers, fruits, and feathers were among the popular adornments for headgear of the day), she knew, could collectively speak volumes about a woman's wealth, class, age, and degree of virtue or modesty.

Fashions in Europe at end of the eighteenth century and the beginning of the nineteenth took a decided turn away from the lavish brocades and powdered wigs that had previously prevailed, and toward the simple and informal. For men, breeches became longer and were usually tucked into boots, and high-collared linen shirts were worn with cravats tied in various manners. For women, corsets were temporarily set aside and replaced by a high-waisted, more natural silhouette, modeled on the garments sported by classical Greek and Roman statuary. Muslin, a sheer, flowing fabric that draped well and was easy to wash and care for, perfectly fit the bill. Despite this somewhat more "relaxed" style of dressing, it was still considered racy for a woman to leave the house without a head covering of some sort. As Jane wrote to her sister in 1796, "We went in our two Carriages to Nackington; but how we divided, I shall leave you to surmise, merely observing that as Eliz: and I were without

Hat or Bonnet, it would not have been very convenient for us to go in the Chair."

Jane and her sister were often short of money, so keeping their wardrobes fresh was never easy, as, again, her letters show. Regardless of that handicap, though, the two were considered to be somewhat "fashion challenged," according to her niece Anna Lefroy, in that they took to dressing a bit stodgily at a fairly young age. During Austen's time, caps were usually worn by older or married women, household servants, and children—everyone, really, except young ladies—but Jane apparently wore them at the age of twenty-three, as she does in the single surviving sketch that we have of her, done by her sister, and apparently not a very true or a very flattering likeness of the tall, slim, hazel-eyed and brunette Austen. Doubtless Jane would have preferred a better image of herself to be left to the world; though she often adopted an amused and rather sardonic tone regarding the vanities of appearance and dress, she was, like most women, well aware of the powers of beauty and did her best to steer clear of a "state of Inelegance."

I took the liberty a few days ago of asking your Black velvet Bonnet to lend me its cawl, which it very readily did, & by which I have been enabled to give a considerable improvement of dignity to my Cap, which was before too *nidgetty* to please me.

—*from a letter to her sister, Cassandra, December 18–19, 1798*

*   *   *

At fifteen, appearances were mending; she began to curl her hair and long for balls; her complexion improved; her features were softened by plumpness and color, her eyes gained more animation, and her figure more consequence. Her love of dirt gave way to an inclination for finery, and she grew clean as she grew smart; she now had the pleasure of sometimes hearing her mother and father remark on her personal improvement. "Catherine grows quite a good-looking girl,—she is almost pretty today," were words which caught her ears now and then;

and how welcome were the sounds! To look *almost* pretty, is an acquisition of higher delight to a girl who has been looking plain the first fifteen years of her life, than a beauty from her cradle can ever receive.

—*on Catherine Morland, in* Northanger Abbey

* * *

"*She*, a beauty! I should as soon call her mother a wit!"

—*Mr. Darcy, on Elizabeth Bennet, in* Pride and Prejudice

* * *

Dress is at all times a frivolous distinction, and excessive solicitude about it often destroys its own aim. Catherine knew all this very well . . . and yet she lay awake ten minutes on Wednesday night debating between her spotted and her tamboured [embroidered] muslin and nothing but the shortness of the time prevented her from buying a new one for the evening. This would have been an error in judgment, great though not uncommon, from which one of the other sex, rather than her own, a brother rather than a great aunt, might have warned her,

for man only can be aware of the insensibility of man towards a new gown. It would be mortifying to the feelings of many ladies, could they be made to understand
how little the heart of man is affected by what is costly
or new in their attire; how little it is biassed by the tex-
ture of their muslin, and how unsusceptible of peculiar
tenderness towards the spotted, the sprigged, the mull
or the jackonet [types of muslin].

—on *Catherine Morland, in* Northanger Abbey

✳   ✳   ✳

Next week [I] shall begin my operations on my hat,
on which You know my principal hopes of happiness
depend.

—*from a letter to her sister, Cassandra,*
  October 27–28, 1798

✳   ✳   ✳

Marianne was still handsomer [than was Elinor]. Her
form, though not so correct as her sister's, in having the
advantage of height, was more striking; and her face was

so lovely, that when, in the common cant of praise, she was called a beautiful girl, truth was less violently outraged than usually happens.

—*on Marianne Dashwood, in* Sense and Sensibility

* * *

Charlotte & I did my hair, which I fancy looked very indifferent; nobody abused it however, & I retired delighted with my success.

—*from a letter to her sister, Cassandra, November 1, 1800*

* * *

. . . that you should meditate the purchase of a new muslin Gown [is a] delightful [circumstance].—*I am determined to buy a handsome one whenever I can, & I am so tired & ashamed of half my present stock that I even blush at the sight of the wardrobe which contains them.*

—*from a letter to her sister, Cassandra,*

December 24–26, 1798

* * *

"But he talked of flannel waistcoats," said Marianne; "and with me a flannel waistcoat is invariably connected with aches, cramps, rheumatisms, and every species of ailment that can affect the old and the feeble."

—*Marianne Dashwood on Colonel Brandon, in* Sense
   and Sensibility

*   *   *

I have changed my mind, & changed the trimmings on my Cap this morning; they are now such as you suggested;—I felt as if I should not prosper if I strayed from your directions, & I think it makes me look more like Lady Conyngham now than it did before, which is all that one lives for now.

—*from a letter to her sister, Cassandra,*
   December 18–19, 1798

*   *   *

Sir Walter, without hesitation, declared the Admiral to be the best-looking sailor he had ever met with, and went so far as to say, that if his own man might have had the arranging of his hair, he should not be ashamed of being seen with him anywhere.

—*on Sir Walter Elliot and Admiral Croft, in* Persuasion

* * *

Flowers are very much worn, & Fruit is still more the thing.—Eliz: has a bunch of Strawberries, & I have seen Grapes, Cherries, Plumbs & Apricots—There are likewise Almonds & raisins, french plums & Tamarinds at the Grocers, but I have never seen any of them in hats.

—*from a letter to her sister, Cassandra, June 2, 1799*

* * *

[Willoughby's] manly beauty and more than common gracefulness were instantly the theme of general admiration, and the laugh which his gallantry raised against Marianne received particular spirit from his exterior attractions. Marianne herself had seen less of his person than the rest, for the confusion which crimsoned over her face, on his lifting her up, had robbed her of the power of regarding him after their entering the house.

But she had seen enough of him to join in all the admiration of the others, and with an energy which always adorned her praise. His person and air were equal to what her fancy had ever drawn for the hero of a favorite story . . . Every circumstance belonging to him was interesting . . . and she soon found out that of all manly dresses a shooting-jacket was the most becoming.

  —*on Willoughby, upon his having rescued Marianne*
    Dashwood after a fall, in Sense and Sensibility

*   *   *

Now I will give you the history of Mary's veil . . . I had no difficulty in getting a muslin veil for half a guinea, & not much more in discovering afterwards that the Muslin was thick, dirty & ragged, and would therefore by no means do for a united Gift.—I changed it consequently as soon as I could, & considering what a state my imprudence had reduced me to, I thought myself lucky in getting a black Lace one for 16 shillings—. I hope the half of that sum will not greatly exceed what

You had intended to offer up on the altar of Sister-in-law affection.

—*from a letter to her sister, Cassandra, June 11, 1799*

*   *   *

It sometimes happens, that a woman is handsomer at twenty-nine than she was ten years before; and, generally speaking, if there has been neither ill health nor anxiety, it is a time of life at which scarcely any charm is lost.

—*on Elizabeth Elliot, in* Persuasion

*   *   *

What dreadful Hot weather we have!—It keeps one in a continual state of Inelegance.

—*from a letter to her sister, Cassandra, September 18, 1796*

*   *   *

"Muslin can never be said to be wasted. I have heard my sister say so forty times, when she has been extravagant in buying more than she wanted, or careless in cutting it to pieces."

    —*Henry Tilney to Catherine Morland and Mrs. Allen, in*
      Northanger Abbey

*   *   *

I am nursing myself up now into as beautiful a state as I can, because I hear that Dr White means to call on me before he leaves the Country.

    —*from a letter to her sister, Cassandra,*
      September 8–9, 1816

*   *   *

"Your conjecture is totally wrong, I assure you. My mind was more agreeably engaged. I have been meditating on the very great pleasure which a pair of fine eyes in the face of a pretty woman can bestow."

    —*Mr. Darcy to Miss Bingley, about Elizabeth Bennet, in*
      Pride and Prejudice

*   *   *

Though you have given me unlimited powers concerning Your Sprig, I cannot determine what to do about it, & shall therefore in this & every future letter continue to ask you for further directions. . . . I cannot help thinking that it is more natural to have flowers grow out of the head than fruit.—What do you think on that subject?

—*from a letter to her sister, Cassandra, June 11, 1799*

✻ ✻ ✻

VANITY AND
OTHER VICES

~~~

*J*udging from her written words, Jane Austen prized the qualities of good conduct and good sense beyond most others; and while her heroes and heroines may require some knowledge and experience to hone these qualities, they invariably do so by novel's end. Moral character is, in her books, a serious concern—and not surprisingly so. Austen's work was influenced by a number of different literary traditions that were prevalent in the eighteenth century. Scholars tend to agree that her books most closely follow in the tradition of writers such as Samuel Richardson, Henry Fielding, and Fanny Burney, in that they center around situations in which moral questions and situations come into play. Though liberally mixing in a strong dose of satire, Austen's main focus is on her heroines' and heroes' psychological and moral struggles, as they stumble their way toward marital bliss—the outward sign, in Austen's world, of inner growth.

One strong influence on Austen's tendency to especially prize the qualities of rational thinking and behavior was something called the Age (or Cult) of Sensibility, which took place in England during the mid- to late eighteenth century. Basically, this was a movement that emphasized feeling and emotion over rational thinking as a guide to moral behavior. The movement gave rise to a genre of writing called "sentimental" literature, with which Austen was quite familiar, and which she parodied brilliantly as a young writer. Her later writing shows her continued concern with promoting reason and sense over excesses of emotionalism—most obviously in *Sense and Sensibility*, but in her other novels as well.

The transformation that was taking place in England during her lifetime likely exerted an influence on Austen's concern with morality as well. Agriculture was being replaced, to a large degree, with industry, and cities were growing larger and more populous. While London became a grand and spectacular example of modern design and ingenuity, it was also teeming with the poor and downtrodden, and was, to many minds, synonymous with vice and sin. "Here I am once more in this Scene of Dissipation & vice, and I begin already to find my Morals corrupted," Austen wrote to her sister, Cassandra, upon arriving in London in August 1796. Though her tone here is obviously arch, she seems to have subscribed to some of the prevailing thought of her day that rural life promoted good health—morally and spiritually as well as physically. (Her most exemplary characters tend to be fond of walking and nature—and not opposed to getting a bit down and dirty now and then—while those less admirable have no time or taste for either.)

Many of Austen's characters, of course, rate rather pitifully on the moral Richter scale. And thank goodness, since it's around these more "flawed" individuals that so much of Austen's comedy revolves. Vanity, pride, envy, narcissism, cruelty, greed, dishonesty, ignorance, sloth, silliness, and plain old stupidity—Austen exposes the gamut of human frailties in all their glory and absurdity more memorably and divertingly than all but a handful of other writers before her time or since.

"Vanity and pride are different things, though the words are often used synonymously. A person may be proud without being vain. Pride relates more to our opinion of ourselves, vanity to what we would have others think of us."

—*Mary Bennet, in* Pride and Prejudice

*　*　*

Elinor saw, with concern, the excess of her sister's sensibility; but by Mrs. Dashwood it was valued and cherished. They encouraged each other now in the violence of their affliction. The agony of grief which overpowered them at first, was voluntarily renewed, was sought for, was created again and again. They gave themselves up wholly to their sorrow, seeking increase of wretchedness in every reflection that could afford it, and resolved against ever admitting consolation in future.

—*on Elinor Dashwood, her sister Marianne, and their mother, in* Sense and Sensibility

＊ ＊ ＊

"His pride," said Miss Lucas, "does not offend *me* so much as pride often does, because there is an excuse for it. One cannot wonder that so very fine a young man, with family, fortune, everything in his favor, should think highly of himself. If I may so express it, he has a *right* to be proud."

"That is very true," replied Elizabeth, "and I could easily forgive *his* pride, if he had not mortified *mine*."

—*Charlotte Lucas and Elizabeth Bennet, about Mr. Darcy, in* Pride and Prejudice

＊ ＊ ＊

"Vanity working on a weak head produces every sort of mischief."

—*Mr. Knightley to Emma Woodhouse in* Emma

* * *

"Nothing is more deceitful than the appearance of humility. It is often only carelessness of opinion, and sometimes an indirect boast."

—*Mr. Darcy to Elizabeth Bennet, in* Pride and Prejudice

* * *

"Selfishness must always be forgiven, you know, because there is no hope of a cure."

—*Mary Crawford to Fanny Price, in* Mansfield Park

* * *

Vanity was the beginning and the end of Sir Walter Elliot's character; vanity of person and of situation. He had been remarkably handsome in his youth; and, at fifty-four, was still a very fine man. Few women could think more of their personal appearance than he did; nor could the valet of any new-made lord be more delighted with the place he held in society. He considered the blessing of beauty as inferior only to the blessing of a baronetcy;

and the Sir Walter Elliot, who united these gifts, was the constant object of his warmest respect and devotion.

His good looks and his rank had one fair claim on his attachment; since to them he must have owed a wife of very superior character to anything deserved by his own.

—*from* Persuasion

* * *

"I do not defend him . . . But this I will say, that his fault, a liking to make girls a little in love with him, is not half so dangerous to a wife's happiness, as a tendency to fall in love himself, which he has never been addicted to."

—*Mary Crawford, about her brother Henry, to Fanny*
  Price, in Mansfield Park

* * *

"You take delight in vexing me. You have no compassion on my poor nerves."

"You mistake me, my dear. I have a high respect for your nerves. They are my old friends. I have heard you mention them with consideration these twenty years at least."

—*Mrs. Bennet and Mr. Bennet, in* Pride and Prejudice

*   *   *

Mr. Collins was not a sensible man, and the deficiency of nature had been but little assisted by education or society; . . . The subjection in which his father had brought him up, had given him originally great humility of manner, but it was now a good deal counteracted by the self-conceit of a weak head, living in retirement, and the consequential feelings of early and unexpected prosperity. A fortunate chance had recommended him to Lady Catherine de Bourgh . . . and the respect which he felt for her high rank, and his veneration for her as his patroness, mingling with a very good opinion of himself, of his authority as a clergyman, and his rights as a rector, made him altogether a mixture of pride and obsequiousness, self-importance and humility.

—*from* Pride and Prejudice

* * *

He had vanity, which strongly inclined him, in the first place, to think she did love him, though she might not know it herself; and which, secondly, when constrained at last to admit that she did not know her own present feelings, convinced him that he should be able in time to make those feelings what he wished.

—*on Henry Crawford and Fanny Price, in*
Mansfield Park

* * *

He was not an ill-disposed young man, unless to be rather cold hearted and rather selfish, is to be ill-disposed . . .

—*on John Dashwood, in* Sense and Sensibility

* * *

"Has [Miss de Bourgh] been presented? I do not remember her name among the ladies at court."

"Her indifferent state of health unhappily prevents her being in town; and by that means, as I told Lady Catherine myself one day, has deprived the British court of its brightest ornament. Her ladyship seemed pleased with the idea, and you may imagine that I am happy on every occasion to offer those little delicate compliments which are always acceptable to ladies. I have more than once observed to Lady Catherine that her charming daughter seemed born to be a duchess, and that the most elevated rank, instead of giving her consequence, would be adorned by her.—These are the kind of little things which please her ladyship, and it is a sort of attention which I conceive myself peculiarly bound to pay."

"You judge very properly," said Mr. Bennet, "and it is happy for you that you possess the talent of flattering with delicacy. May I ask whether these pleasing attentions proceed from the impulse of the moment, or are the result of previous study?"

"They arise chiefly from what is passing at the time, and though I sometimes amuse myself with suggesting and arranging such little elegant compliments as may be adapted to ordinary occasions, I always wish to give them as unstudied an air as possible."

—*Mr. Collins and Mr. Bennet, in* Pride and Prejudice

* * *

"Jemima has just told me that the butcher says there is a bad sore-throat very much about. I dare say I shall catch it; and my sore-throats, you know, are always worse than anybody's."

—*Mary Musgrove, in a letter to Anne Elliot, in* Persuasion

* * *

Mrs. John Dashwood saw the packages depart with a sigh: she could not help feeling it hard that as Mrs. Dashwood's income would be so trifling in comparison with their own, she should have any handsome article of furniture.

—*from* Sense and Sensibility

* * *

Sir Edward's great object in life was to be seductive.— With such personal advantage as he knew himself to possess, and such talents as he did also give himself credit for, he regarded it as his duty.—He felt that he was formed to be a dangerous man—quite in the lines of the Lovelaces.—The very name of "Sir Edward," he thought, carried some degree of fascination with it.

—*from* Sanditon, *an unfinished novel begun by Austen*
   shortly before she died, also called The Brothers

*   *   *

"My love, you contradict everybody," said his wife with her usual laugh. "Do you know that you are quite rude?"

"I did not know I contradicted anybody in calling your mother ill-bred."

—*Mrs. Palmer and Mr. Palmer, in* Sense and Sensibility

*   *   *

"You ought certainly to forgive them as a Christian, but never to admit them in your sight, or allow their names to be mentioned in your hearing."

—*Mr. Collins to the Bennets, about Lydia Bennet's "sad*
   business" with Mr. Wickham, in Pride and Prejudice

* * *

To his wife he was very little otherwise indebted, than as her ignorance and folly had contributed to his amusement.

—*on Mr. Bennet, in* Pride and Prejudice

* * *

OTHER PEOPLE

⸎

"For what do we live, but to make sport for our neighbors, and laugh at them in our turn?" The line is Mr. Bennet's, in *Pride in Prejudice,* but the sentiment is, at least to some degree, Jane Austen's own. She could easily have penned it in one of her many letters to her sister, Cassandra, where she took great pleasure in observation as a sport, constantly turning her keen eye (and setting the power of her witty pen) on her neighbors, her friends, her family, and anyone else who crossed her path. And while of course a great many individuals did earn her warm praise and genuine admiration, no one was too old, too young, or in any way too sacred to be mirthfully sent up for her sister's and her own amusement.

"Whenever I fall into misfortune," she wrote to Cassandra in January 1799, "how many jokes it ought to furnish to my acquaintance in general, or I shall die dreadfully in their debt for entertainment."

In all fairness, though, Austen laughed at herself as often as she laughed at others; her letters are full of breezy self-mockery, about her looks, her age, and even her writing. It should be noted, too, that Austen's humorous observations were never meant to be shared with anyone but Cassandra.

There were very few Beauties, & such as there were, were not very handsome. Miss Iremonger did not look well, & Mrs Blount was the only one much admired. She appeared exactly as she did in September, with the same broad face, diamond bandeau, white shoes, pink husband, & fat neck.—The two Miss Coxes were there; I traced in one the remains of the vulgar, broad-featured girl who danced at Enham eight years ago;—the other is refined into a nice, composed looking girl. . . . The Miss Maitlands are both prettyish; very like Anne; with brown skins, large dark eyes, & a good deal of nose.—The General has got the Gout, & Mrs Maitland the Jaundice.—Miss Debary, Susan & Sally all in black . . . made their appearance, & I was as civil to them as their bad breath would allow me.

—*from a letter to her sister, Cassandra, November 20–21, 1800*

* * *

Good Mrs Deedes!—I hope she will get the better of this Marianne [her newly born eighteenth child], & then I w^d recommend to her & Mr D. the simple regimen of separate rooms.

—*from a letter to her niece Fanny Knight,*
  February 20–21, 1817

* * *

Miss H. is an elegant, pleasing, pretty looking girl, about 19 I suppose, or 19 & ½, or 19 & ¼, with flowers in her head, & Music at her fingers ends.—She plays very well indeed. I have seldom heard anybody with more pleasure.

—*from a letter to her sister, Cassandra, May 29, 1811*

✳ ✳ ✳

. . . & at the bottom of Kingsdown Hill we met a Gentleman in a Buggy, who on a minute examination
turned out to be Dr Hall—& Dr Hall in such very deep
mourning that either his Mother, his Wife, or himself
must be dead.

—*from a letter to her sister, Cassandra, May 17, 1799*

✳ ✳ ✳

Charles Powlett gave a dance on Thursday, to the great
disturbance of all his neighbours, of course, who, you
know, take a most lively interest in the state of his fi-
nances, and live in hopes of his being soon ruined.

—*from a letter to her sister, Cassandra, December 1–2, 1798*

✳ ✳ ✳

Mrs Harding is a goodlooking woman, but not much like
Mrs Toke, inasmuch as she is very brown & has scarcely
any teeth . . .

—*from a letter to her sister, Cassandra, May 29, 1811*

* * *

Mrs F. A. seldom either looks or appears well.—Little Embryo is troublesome I suppose.

—from a letter to her sister, Cassandra, September 8–9, 1816

* * *

If Miss Pearson should return with me, pray be careful not to expect too much Beauty.

—from a letter to her sister, Cassandra, September 18, 1796

* * *

A handsome young Man certainly, with quiet, gentle-manlike manners.—I set him down as sensible rather than Brilliant.—There is nobody Brilliant nowadays.

—from a letter to her sister, Cassandra, September 23–24, 1813

* * *

I wondered whether you happened to see Mr Blackall's marriage in the Papers last Jan^ry. *We* did. He was married at Clifton to a Miss Lewis. . . . I should very much like to know what sort of a Woman she is. He was a piece of Perfection, noisy Perfection himself which I always rec-ollect with regard. . . . I would wish Miss Lewis to be of a silent turn & rather ignorant, but naturally intelligent & wishing to learn;—fond of cold veal pies, green tea in the afternoon, & a green window blind at night.

—*from a letter to her brother Francis, July 3–6, 1813*

* * *

. . . I am proud to say that I have a very good eye at an Adultress, for tho' repeatedly assured that another in the same party was the *She,* I fixed upon the right one from the first. . . . She is not so pretty as I expected; her face has the same defect of baldness as her sister's, & her features not so handsome;—she was highly rouged, & looked rather quietly & contentedly silly than anything else.

—*from a letter to her sister, Cassandra, May 12–13, 1801*

* * *

Dr Gardiner was married yesterday to Mrs Percy & her three daughters.

—from a letter to her sister, Cassandra, June 11, 1799

* * *

There are two Traits in [Miss Fletcher's] Character which are pleasing; namely, she admires Camilla [Fanny Burney's popular novel of the day], & drinks no cream in her Tea.

—from a letter to her sister, Cassandra, September 15–16, 1796

* * *

I had the comfort of finding out the other evening who all the fat girls with short noses were that disturbed me at the 1st H. Ball. They all prove to be Miss Atkinsons of Enham.

—from a letter to her sister, Cassandra, November 20–21, 1800

* * *

Mrs Hall, of Sherbourn was brought to bed yesterday of a dead child, some weeks before she expected, oweing to a fright.—I suppose she happened unawares to look at her husband.

   —from a letter to her sister, Cassandra,
     October 27–28, 1798

✳   ✳   ✳

Mr Richard Harvey is going to be married; but as it is a great secret, & only known to half the Neighbourhood, you must not mention it.

   —from a letter to her sister, Cassandra, September 5, 1796

✳   ✳   ✳

She found [Lord Craven's] manners very pleasing indeed.—The little flaw of having a Mistress now living with him at Ashdown Park, seems to be the only unpleasing circumstance about him.

   —from a letter to her sister, Cassandra, January 8–9, 1801

✳   ✳   ✳

Mrs Powlett was at once expensively & nakedly dress'd;—we have had the satisfaction of estimating her

Lace & her Muslin; & she said too little to afford us much
other amusement.

—*from a letter to her sister, Cassandra, January 8–9, 1801*

*　*　*

There is no reason to suppose that Miss Morgan is dead
after all.

—*from a letter to her sister, Cassandra, December 1–2, 1798*

*　*　*

FRIENDSHIP

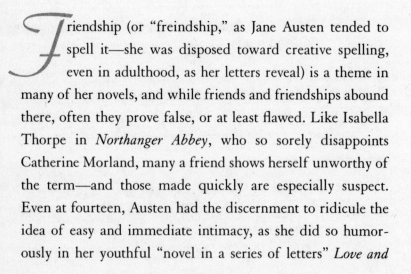

*F*riendship (or "freindship," as Jane Austen tended to spell it—she was disposed toward creative spelling, even in adulthood, as her letters reveal) is a theme in many of her novels, and while friends and friendships abound there, often they prove false, or at least flawed. Like Isabella Thorpe in *Northanger Abbey*, who so sorely disappoints Catherine Morland, many a friend shows herself unworthy of the term—and those made quickly are especially suspect. Even at fourteen, Austen had the discernment to ridicule the idea of easy and immediate intimacy, as she did so humorously in her youthful "novel in a series of letters" *Love and*

Freindship [sic]. "[Sophia and I] flew into each other's arms," she writes in the voice of her heroine, Laura, "and after having exchanged vows of mutual Freindship for the rest of our Lives, instantly unfolded to each other the most inward secrets of our Hearts."

There are, of course, true friendships depicted in Austen's work. Catherine Morland loses the two-faced Isabella Thorpe but gains the admirable Eleanor Tilney—not to mention her brother, Henry, who becomes not just a friend but a spouse. In fact, friends who turn into husbands are more the norm than the exception in Austen's work. Edmund Bertram is Fanny Price's dearest friend and protector (as well as her first cousin and, in some respects, her "brother"), long before he figures out that he's in love with her. Mr. Knightley is an old family friend of Emma Woodhouse's (and is her brother-in-law, too). Even the pairing of Captain Wentworth and Anne Elliot, despite the passion of the captain's confessional letter (one of the most emotional outpourings of love in all of Austen's work), is described by the author more than once as containing elements of friendship. True friendship, Austen suggests, with its attendant qualities of mutual caring and respect, is the best foundation for love.

Austen was particularly big on the joys of female friendships—no surprise, given her devotion to her sister, Cassandra, who could certainly be called her lifelong best friend. She often depicted the relationship between sisters as such: witness Elizabeth and Jane Bennet in *Pride and Prejudice*, Elinor and Marianne Dashwood in *Sense and Sensibility,* and even Fanny Price and Susan—who, alas, had to wait until chapter 40 to enjoy their sisterly bond in *Mansfield Park*.

Friendship is certainly the finest balm for the pangs of disappointed love.

—*from* Northanger Abbey

* * *

Captain Wentworth, without saying a word, turned to her, and quietly obliged her to be assisted into the carriage.

Yes; he had done it. She was in the carriage, and felt that he had placed her there, that his will and his hands had done it, that she owed it to his perception of her fatigue, and his resolution to give her rest. She was very much affected by the view of his disposition towards her, which all these things made apparent. This little circumstance seemed the completion of all that had gone before. She understood him. He could not forgive her, but he could not be unfeeling. Though condemning her for the past, and considering it with high and unjust resentment, though perfectly careless of her, and though becoming attached to another, still he could not see her suffer, without the desire of giving her relief. It was a remainder of former sentiment; it was an impulse of pure, though unacknowledged friendship; it was a proof of his own warm and amiable heart, which she could not contemplate without emotions so compounded of pleasure and pain, that she knew not which prevailed.

—on *Captain Wentworth and Anne Elliot, in* Persuasion

* * *

"Mr. Wickham is blessed with such happy manners as may ensure his making friends; whether he may be equally capable of retaining them is less certain."

—*Mr. Darcy to Elizabeth Bennet, in* Pride and Prejudice

* * *

She was heartily ashamed of her ignorance. A misplaced shame. Where people wish to attach, they should always be ignorant. To come with a well-informed mind is to come with an inability of administering to the vanity of others, which a sensible person would always wish to avoid. A woman especially, if she have the misfortune of knowing anything, should conceal it as well as she can.

—*on Catherine Morland, in* Northanger Abbey

* * *

Harriet certainly was not clever, but she had a sweet, docile, grateful disposition, was totally free from conceit, and only desiring to be guided by anyone she looked up to. Her early attachment to [Emma] herself was very amiable; and her inclination for good company, and power of appreciating what was elegant and clever, showed that there was no want of taste, though strength of understanding must not be expected. Altogether she was quite convinced of Harriet Smith's being exactly the young friend she wanted—exactly the something which her home required.

—*on Harriet Smith and Emma Woodhouse, in* Emma

* * *

"There is so little real friendship in the world!"
—*Mrs. Smith to Anne Elliot, in* Persuasion

* * *

After having been deprived during the course of 3 weeks of a real friend . . . imagine my transports at beholding one most truly worthy of the Name. Sophia was rather above the middle size; most elegantly formed. A soft languor spread over her lovely features, but increased their Beauty.—It was the Characteristic of her Mind.— She was all Sensibility and Feeling. We flew into each

other's arms and after having exchanged vows of mutual
Freindship for the rest of our Lives, instantly unfolded to
each other the most inward secrets of our Hearts.

—*as narrated by Laura in* Love and Freindship [sic]:
A novel in a series of Letters, *a work from*
Austen's juvenilia

* * *

There was a kind of cold-hearted selfishness on both
sides, which mutually attracted them; and they sympa-
thized with each other in an insipid propriety of de-
meanor, and a general want of understanding.

—*on Lady Middleton and Mrs. Dashwood, in*
Sense and Sensibility

* * *

The Hattons' & Milles' dine here today . . . Luckily the
pleasures of Friendship, of unreserved Conversation, of
similarity of Taste & Opinions, will make good amends
for Orange Wine.

—*from a letter to her sister, Cassandra, June 30–July 1, 1808*

* * *

Their conversations turned upon those subjects, of
which the free discussion has generally much to do in
perfecting a sudden intimacy between two young ladies;
such as dress, balls, flirtations, and quizzes. Miss
Thorpe, however, being four years older than Miss Morland, and at least four years better informed, had a very
decided advantage in discussing such points; she could
compare the balls of Bath with those of Tunbridge, its
fashions with the fashions of London; could rectify the
opinions of her new friend in many articles of tasteful attire; could discover a flirtation between any gentleman
and lady who only smiled on each other; and point out a
quiz through the thickness of a crowd. These powers received due admiration from Catherine, to whom they
were entirely new; and the respect which they naturally
inspired might have been too great for familiarity, had
not the easy gaiety of Miss Thorpe's manners, and her
frequent expressions of delight on this acquaintance
with her, softened down every feeling of awe, and left

nothing but tender affection. Their increasing attachment was not to be satisfied with half a dozen turns in the pump-room, but required, when they all quitted it together, that Miss Thorpe should accompany Miss Morland to the very door of Mr. Allen's house; and that they should there part with a most affectionate and lengthened shake of hands, after learning, to their mutual relief, that they should see each other across the theater at night, and say their prayers in the same chapel the next morning.

—*Isabella Thorpe and Catherine Morland, in*
   Northanger Abbey

* * *

This long letter, full of my own concerns alone, will be enough to tire even the friendship of a Fanny.

—*Edmund Bertram, in a letter to Fanny Price, in*
   Mansfield Park

* * *

". . . I wish you knew Miss Andrews, you would be delighted with her . . . I think her beautiful as an angel, and I am so vexed with the men for not admiring her! I scold them all amazingly about it."

"Scold them! Do you scold them for not admiring her?"

"Yes, that I do. There is nothing I would not do for those who are really my friends. I have no notion of loving people by halves; it is not my nature. My attachments are always excessively strong. I told Captain Hunt, at one of our assemblies this winter, that if he was to tease me all night, I would not dance with him, unless he would allow Miss Andrews to be as beautiful as an angel. The men think us incapable of real friendship, you know; and I am determined to show them the difference. Now if I were to hear anybody speak slightingly of you, I should fire up in a moment: but that is not at all likely, for *you* are just the kind of girl to be a great favorite with the men."

"Oh, dear!" cried Catherine, coloring, "how can you say so?" "I know you very well. You have so much

animation, which is exactly what Miss Andrews wants;
for I must confess, there is something amazingly insipid about her . . ."

   —Isabella Thorpe and Catherine Morland, in
     Northanger Abbey

*   *   *

It would be needless to say, that the gentlemen advanced
in the good opinion of each other, as they advanced in
each other's acquaintance, for it could not be otherwise.
Their resemblance in good principles and good sense, in
disposition and manner of thinking, would probably
have been sufficient to unite them in friendship, without
any other attraction; but their being in love with two sisters, and two sisters fond of each other, made that mutual
regard inevitable and immediate, which might otherwise
have waited the effect of time and judgment.

   —on Edward Ferrars and Colonel Brandon, in
     Sense and Sensibility

*   *   *

Miss Fletcher and I were very thick, but I am the thinnest of the two.

—*from a letter to her sister, Cassandra, September 15–16, 1796*

* * *

"I can think only of the friends I am leaving: my excellent sister, yourself, and the Bertrams in general. You have all so much more *heart* among you than one finds in the world at large. You all give me a feeling of being able to trust and confide in you, which in common intercourse one knows nothing of."

—*Mary Crawford to Fanny Price, in* Mansfield Park

* * *

. . . hardly had she been seated ten minutes before a lady of about her own age, who was sitting by her, and had been looking at her attentively for several minutes, addressed her with great complaisance in these words:—"I think, I cannot be mistaken; it is a long time since I had the pleasure of seeing you, but is not your name Allen?" This question answered, as it readily was, the stranger pronounced hers to be Thorpe; and Mrs. Allen immediately recognized the features of a former schoolfellow and intimate, whom she had seen only once since their respective marriages, and that many years ago. Their joy on this meeting was very great, as well it might, since they had been contented to know nothing of each other for the past fifteen years. Compliments on good looks now passed; and, after observing how time had slipped away since they were last together, how little they had thought of meeting in Bath, and what a pleasure it was to see an old friend, they proceeded to make inquiries and give intelligence as to their families, sisters, and cousins, talking both together, far more ready to give than receive information, and each hearing very little of what the other said.

—*from* Northanger Abbey

* * *

"It is such a happiness when good people get together— and they always do."

—*Miss Bates, in* Emma

* * *

THE SEXES

⁂

*A*usten had as much fun as any present-day novelist, and more fun than most, in her depiction of men and women, and the (sometimes) irreconcilable differences between them. ("If there is anything disagreeable going on," Mary Musgrove complains to Anne Elliot in *Persuasion,* "men are sure to get out of it"). At the same time, though, Austen's portrayal of the sexes expresses more serious concerns about her society's treatment and view of women: Not only were they completely lacking in legal rights (which was certainly bad enough) but they were routinely acknowledged to be mindless, or at best irrational, creatures.

"I hate to hear you talking so . . . as if women were all fine ladies, instead of rational creatures," says Mrs. Croft to her brother Frederick Wentworth in *Persuasion*. Her plea is very much like that of Elizabeth Bennet to Mr. Collins in *Pride and Prejudice*: "Do not consider me now as an elegant female intending to plague you, but as a rational creature speaking the truth from my heart." Add to this Austen's point, expressed in *Northanger Abbey* (obviously only somewhat tongue-in-cheek), that "imbecility in females is a great enhancement of their personal charms," and it becomes clear: For all her desire to amuse her readers, Austen was also taking what was then quite a bold stand in attempting to promote better views, understanding, and treatment of her sex in the male-dominated world in which she lived. All the heroines of her novels (strong, rational women, who, if a bit wrong-headed, spoiled, or cocky at the start, think through their situations and learn from their experiences) make their own decisions about whom to marry—economically, socially, and in every other respect the most important decision of their lives. This was a monumental thing in Austen's day.

Austen had her sympathies for men, too, of course, and especially for younger brothers, who had a tough lot in life themselves, because of the laws by which eldest sons routinely inherited their family's estate. She also knew that a system that lacked freedoms for women—which left them totally at the mercy of the men of the family—had a second level of evil, in that it left the men to bear the burden of their widowed mothers and unmarried sisters, and younger brothers often to have to marry women with large dowries whether they cared for them or not.

In such a world, it's remarkable that Austen managed to find as much humor as she did in the subject of the sexes. A masterful satirist from an early age, she understood the power of humor to instruct, and to bring about change. No doubt, too, she just found men and women funny.

The ladies probably exchanged looks which meant, "Men never know when things are dirty or not," and the gentlemen perhaps thought each to himself, "Women will have their little nonsenses and needless cares."

—*from* Emma

* * *

"And now Henry . . . you may as well make Miss Morland understand yourself—unless you mean to have her think you . . . a great brute in your opinion of women. . . . Miss Morland is not used to your odd ways."

"I shall be most happy to make her better acquainted with them."

"No doubt;—but that is no explanation of the present."

"What am I to do?"

"You know what you ought to do. Clear your character handsomely before her. Tell her that you think very highly of the understanding of women."

"Miss Morland, I think very highly of all the women in the world—especially of those—whoever they may be—with whom I happen to be in company."

"That is not enough. Be more serious."

"Miss Morland, no one can think more highly of the understanding of women than I do. In my opinion, nature has given them so much, that they never find it necessary to use more than half."

—*Eleanor Tilney to her brother Henry, and Henry in turn to Catherine Morland, in* Northanger Abbey

* * *

". . . I have a very poor opinion of young men who live in Derbyshire; and their intimate friends who live in Hertfordshire are not much better. I am sick of them all. Thank Heaven! I am going tomorrow where I shall find a man who has not one agreeable quality, who has neither manner nor sense to recommend him. Stupid ones are the only ones worth knowing after all."

—*Elizabeth Bennet to her aunt Mrs. Gardiner, on Mr. Wickham and Mr. Collins, in* Pride and Prejudice

* * *

"I am really not tired, which I almost wonder at; for we must have walked at least a mile in this wood. Do you not think we have?"

"Not half a mile," was his sturdy answer; for he was not yet so much in love as to measure distance, or reckon time, with feminine lawlessness.

—*Mary Crawford and Edmund Bertram, in* Mansfield Park

* * *

"I have sometimes thought," said Catherine, doubtingly, "whether ladies do write so much better letters than gentlemen! That is—I should not think the superiority was always on our side."

"As far as I have had the opportunity of judging, it appears to me that the usual style of letter-writing among women is faultless, except in three particulars."

"And what are they?"

"A general deficiency of subject, a total inattention to stops, and a very frequent ignorance of grammar."

—*Catherine Morland and Henry Tilney, in*

Northanger Abbey

* * *

"It is amazing to me," said Bingley, "how young ladies can have patience to be so very accomplished as they all are."

"All young ladies accomplished? My dear Charles, what do you mean?"

"Yes, all of them, I think. They all paint tables, cover screens, and net purses. I scarcely know any one who cannot do all this, and I am sure I never heard a young lady spoken of for the first time without being informed that she was very accomplished."

"Your list of the common extent of accomplishments," said Darcy, "has too much truth. The word is applied to many a woman who deserves it no otherwise than by netting a purse or covering a screen. But I am very far from agreeing with you in your estimation of ladies in general. I cannot boast of knowing more than half a dozen, in the whole range of my acquaintance, that are really accomplished."

"Nor I, I am sure," said Miss Bingley.

"Then," observed Elizabeth, "you must comprehend a great deal in your idea of an accomplished woman."

"Yes; I do comprehend a great deal in it."

"Oh! certainly," cried his faithful assistant, "no one can really be esteemed accomplished who does not greatly surpass what is usually met with. A woman must have a thorough knowledge of music, singing, drawing, dancing, and the modern languages, to deserve the word; and besides all this, she must possess a certain something in her air and manner of walking, the tone of her voice, her address and expressions, or the word will be but half deserved."

"All this she must possess," added Darcy, "and to all this she must yet add something more substantial, in the improvement of her mind by extensive reading."

"I am no longer surprised at your knowing *only* six accomplished women. I rather wonder now at your knowing *any*."

—*from* Pride and Prejudice

* * *

". . . As I must therefore conclude that you are not serious in your rejection of me, I shall choose to attribute it to your wish of increasing my love by suspense, according to the usual practice of elegant females."

"I so assure you sir that I have no pretension to that kind of elegance which consists in tormenting a respectable man. I would rather be paid the compliment of being believed sincere. I thank you again and again for the honor you have done me in your proposals, but to accept them is absolutely impossible. My feelings in every respect forbid it. Can I speak plainer? Do not consider me now as an elegant female intending to plague you, but as a rational creature speaking the truth from my heart."

—*Elizabeth Bennet to Mr. Collins, in* Pride and Prejudice

✻　✻　✻

Maria, with only Mr. Rushworth to attend to her, [was] doomed to the repeated details of his day's sports, good or bad, his boast of his dogs, his jealousy of his neighbors, his doubts of their qualifications, and his zeal after poachers—subjects which will not find their way to female feelings without some talent on one side, or some attachment on the other.

 —on *Maria Bertram, in* Mansfield Park

∗ ∗ ∗

". . . What can you have to do with hearts? You men have none of you any hearts."

 "If we have not hearts, we have eyes, and they give us torment enough."

 —*Isabella Thorpe and Captain Tilney, in*
  Northanger Abbey

∗ ∗ ∗

The advantages of natural folly in a beautiful girl have been already set forth by the capital pen of a sister author [this was a reference to Fanny Burney, author of the popular novel *Camilla*]; and to her treatment of the subject I will only add, in justice to men, that though to the larger and more trifling part of the sex, imbecility in females is a great enhancement of their personal charms, there is a portion of them too reasonable and too well informed themselves to desire anything more in women than ignorance.

—*from* Northanger Abbey

* * *

". . . there are certainly not so many men of large fortune in the world, as there are pretty women to deserve them."

—*from* Mansfield Park

* * *

Mrs. Allen was one of that numerous class of females, whose society can raise no other emotion than surprise at there being any men in the world who could like them well enough to marry them.

—*from* Northanger Abbey

* * *

"We [women] certainly do not forget you [men], so soon as you forget us. It is, perhaps, our fate rather than our merit. We cannot help ourselves. We live at home, quiet, confined, and our feelings prey upon us. You are forced on exertion. You have always a profession, pursuits, business of some sort or other, to take you back into the world immediately, and continual occupation and change soon weaken impressions."

"Granting your assertion that the world does this so soon for men, (which, however, I do not think I shall grant), it does not apply to Benwick [Captain Benwick, of whom they have just been speaking]. He has not been forced upon any exertion. The peace turned him on shore at the very moment, and he has been living with us, in our little family-circle, ever since."

"True," said Anne, "very true; I did not recollect. But what shall we say now, Captain Harville? If the change be not from outward circumstances, it must be from within; it must be nature, man's nature, which has done the business for Captain Benwick."

"No, no, it is not man's nature. I will not allow it to be more man's nature than woman's to be inconstant and forget those they do love, or have loved. I believe the reverse. I believe in a true analogy between our bodily frames and our mental; and that as our bodies are the strongest, so are our feelings; capable of bearing most rough usage, and riding out the heaviest weather."

"Your feelings may be the strongest," replied Anne, "but the same spirit of analogy will authorize me to assert that ours are the most tender. Man is more robust than woman, but he is not longer-lived; which exactly explains my view of the nature of their attachments. . . ."

". . . we shall never agree, I suppose, upon this point. No man and woman would, probably. But let me observe that all histories are against you. . . . All stories, prose, and verse. . . . I do not think I ever opened a book in my life which had not something to say about a woman's inconstancy. Songs and proverbs, all talk of woman's fickleness. But perhaps you will say, these were all written by men."

"Perhaps I shall.—Yes, yes, if you please, no reference to examples in books. Men have had every advantage in telling their own story. Education has been theirs in so much higher a degree; the pen has been in their hands. I will not allow books to prove anything."

—*Anne Elliot and Captain Harville, in* Persuasion

* * *

"Is it a pretty place?" asked Catherine.

"What say you, Eleanor? Speak your opinion, for ladies can best tell the taste of ladies in regard to places as well as men."

—*Catherine Morland and General Tilney, to his daughter*
   Eleanor, in Northanger Abbey

* * *

"All the privilege I claim for my own sex (it is not a very enviable one, you need not covet) is that of loving longest, when existence or when hope is gone."

—*Anne Elliot to Captain Harville, in* Persuasion

* * *

Who can understand a young Lady?

—*from a letter to her niece Fanny Knight, March 13, 1817*

* * *

COURTSHIP

Jane Austen's letters, especially those she wrote to her sister, Cassandra, are filled with balls, parties, and social visits, prime backdrops for the business of courting—and it seems as though Jane, who was attractive, clever, and vivacious, had her share of admirers and suitors. "There was one Gentleman, an officer of the Cheshire, a very good looking young Man, who I was told wanted very much to be introduced to me;—" she wrote to Cassandra after attending a ball in January 1799, "but as he did not want it quite enough to take much trouble in effecting it, We never could bring it about." Other men, though, were more successful in working their way into Jane's company. Austen seems to have had a youthful infatuation with one Edward Taylor, apparently the owner of a pair of "beautiful dark Eyes." In September 1796, she wrote to her sister that she had driven past his family's home and "contemplated with a melancholy pleasure, the abode of Him, on whom I once fondly doated." There were other admirers of that same period, including a Mr. Heartley and Charles Powlett, who, she wrote to her Cassandra, tried to kiss her; apparently, he was disappointed.

In 1798, Mrs. Lefroy, a friend and neighbor who may have felt a bit guilty about the aborted romance between Jane and her nephew Tom (see the chapter "Love"), tried to fix Jane up with the Rev. Samuel Blackall, a Fellow at Cambridge who had expressed an interest in her—but apparently Jane didn't return the interest. As she wrote to her sister, "There seems no likelihood of his coming in to Hampshire this Christmas, and it is therefore most probable that our indifference will soon be mutual, unless his regard, which appeared to spring from knowing nothing of me at first, is best supported by never seeing me." Like her characters, she had her own ideas about who would and would not woo her.

Later in her life, Jane's letters reveal little of any possible suitors she may have had. Instead, she seems to have taken on the role of romantic confidante and adviser to several of her nieces. In 1814, she wrote to her niece Fanny Knight, then twenty-one years old, about a young man she had been seeing: "When I consider how few young Men you have yet seen much of—how capable you are (yes, I do still think you *very* capable) of being really in love—and how full of temptation the next 6 or 7 years of your Life will probably be—(it is the very period of Life for the *strongest* attachments to be formed)—I cannot wish you with your present very cool feelings to devote yourself in honour to him. It is very true that you never may attach another Man, his equal altogether, but if that other Man has the power of attaching you *more*, he will be in your eyes the most perfect."

"There is no charm equal to tenderness of heart . . . There is nothing to be compared to it. Warmth and tenderness of heart, with an affectionate, open manner, will beat all the cleverness of head in the world, for attraction."

—*Emma Woodhouse, in* Emma

* * *

"A lady's imagination is very rapid; it jumps from admiration to love, from love to matrimony, in a moment."

—*Mr. Darcy to Miss Bingley, in* Pride and Prejudice

* * *

[John Thorpe's] manners did not please Catherine; but he was James's friend and Isabella's brother; and her judgment was further bought off by Isabella's assuring her . . . that John thought her the most charming girl in the world. . . . Had she been older or vainer, such attacks might have done little; but, where youth and diffidence are united, it requires uncommon steadiness of reason to resist the attraction of being called the most charming girl in the world . . . and the consequence was that when the two Morlands . . . set off to walk together to Mr. Allen's, and James . . . said, "Well, Catherine, how do you like my friend Thorpe?" instead of answering, as she probably would have done, . . . "I do not like him at all," she directly replied, "I like him very much; he seems very agreeable."

—*from* Northanger Abbey

* * *

"There is so much of gratitude or vanity in almost every attachment, that it is not safe to leave any to itself. We can all begin freely—a slight preference is natural enough; but there are very few of us who have heart enough to be really in love without encouragement. In nine cases out of ten, a woman had better show *more* affection than she feels. Bingley likes your sister undoubtedly; but he may never do more than like her, if she does not help him on . . ."

—*Charlotte Lucas to Elizabeth Bennet, in*
    Pride and Prejudice

* * *

She had reached the age of seventeen without seeing one amiable youth who could call forth her sensibility, without having inspired one real passion, and without having excited even any admiration but what was very moderate and very transient. This was strange indeed! But strange things may be generally accounted for if their cause be fairly searched out. There was not one lord in the neighborhood—no—not even a baronet. There was not one family among their acquaintance who had reared and supported a boy accidentally found at their door—not one young man whose origin was unknown. Her father had no ward, and the squire of the parish had no children.

But when a young lady is to be a heroine, the perverseness of forty surrounding families cannot prevent her. Something must and will happen to throw a hero in her way.

—*on Catherine Morland, in* Northanger Abbey

* * *

"We all know him to be a proud, unpleasant sort of man. But this would be nothing if you really liked him."

—*Elizabeth Bennet's father, speaking to her about Mr. Darcy, in* Pride and Prejudice

* * *

Catherine feared, as she listened to their discourse, that he indulged himself a little too much with the foibles of others.—"What are you of thinking so earnestly?" said he, as they walked back to the ball-room;—"not of your partner, I hope, for, by that shake of your head, your meditations are not satisfactory."

Catherine colored, and said, "I was not thinking of anything."

"That is artful and deep, to be sure; but I had rather be told at once that you will not tell me."

"Well then, I will not."

"Thank you. For now we shall soon be acquainted, as I am authorized to tease you on this subject whenever we meet, and nothing in the world advances intimacy so much."

—*Henry Tilney to Catherine Morland, in*
  Northanger Abbey

* * *

Tell Mary that I make over Mr Heartley & all his Estate to her for her sole use & Benefit in future, & not only him, but all my other Admirers into the bargain wherever she can find them, even the kiss which C. Powlett wanted to give me, as I mean to confine myself in future to Mr Tom Lefroy, for whom I donot care sixpence.

—*from a letter to her sister, Cassandra, January 14–15, 1796*

* * *

Catherine . . . enjoyed her usual happiness with Henry, listening with sparkling eyes to everything he said; and, in finding him irresistible, becoming so herself.

—*on Catherine Morland and Henry Tilney in*
  Northanger Abbey

* * *

". . . when a young man, be he who he will, comes and makes love to a pretty girl, and promises marriage, he has no business to fly off from his word, only because he grows poor, and a richer girl is ready to have him. Why don't he, in such a case, sell his horses, let his house, turn off his servants, and make a thorough reform at once? I warrant you, Miss Marianne would have been ready to wait till matters came round. But that won't do now a-days; nothing in the way of pleasure can ever be given up by the young men of this age."

—*Mrs. Jennings to Elinor Dashwood, about Willoughby and her sister Marianne, in* Sense and Sensibility

* * *

With Tuesday came the agreeable prospect of seeing him again, and for a longer time than hitherto; of judging of his general manners, and by inference, of the meaning of his manners towards herself; of guessing how soon it might be necessary for her to throw coldness into her air; and of fancying what the observations of all those might be, who were now seeing them together for the first time.

—*on Emma Woodhouse, musing on Frank Churchill, in* Emma

* * *

But Catherine did not know her own advantages—did not know that a good-looking girl, with an affectionate heart and a very ignorant mind, cannot fail of attracting a clever young man, unless circumstances are particularly untoward.

   —*on Catherine Morland, in* Northanger Abbey

* * *

"Yes, and I like her the better for [being engaged]. An engaged woman is always more agreeable than a disengaged. . . . All is safe with a lady engaged; no harm can be done."

   —*Henry Crawford, speaking to his sister Mary about Maria*
     Bertram, in Mansfield Park

* * *

"I understand: she is in love with James, and flirts with Frederick."

   "Oh! no, not flirts. A woman in love with one man cannot flirt with another."

   "It is probable that she will neither love so well, nor

flirt so well, as she might do either singly. The gentlemen must each give up a little."

—*Catherine Morland and Henry Tilney, in*
Northanger Abbey

* * *

[Emma] had already satisfied herself that [Mr. Elton]
thought Harriet a beautiful girl, which she trusted . . .
was foundation enough on his side; and on Harriet's
there could be little doubt that the idea of being preferred by him would have all the usual weight and effi-
cacy. And he was really a very pleasing young man, a
young man whom any woman not fastidious might like.
He was reckoned very handsome; his person much admired in general, though not by her, there being a want
of elegance of feature which she could not dispense
with:—but the girl who could be gratified by a Robert
Martin's riding about the country to get walnuts for her
might very well be conquered by Mr. Elton's admiration.

—*on Emma Woodhouse's plans to make a match of Harriet*
Smith and Mr. Elton, in Emma

* * *

Mr. Crawford did not mean to be in any danger; the Miss Bertrams were worth pleasing, and were ready to be pleased; and he began with no object but of making them like him. He did not want them to die of love; but with sense and temper which ought to have made him judge and feel better, he allowed himself great latitude on such points.

—*on Henry Crawford, in* Mansfield Park

* * *

Unaccountable, however, as the circumstances of his release might appear to the whole family, it was certain that Edward was free; and to what purpose that freedom would be employed was easily pre-determined by all;— for after experiencing the blessings of one imprudent engagement, contracted without his mother's consent, as he had already done for more than four years, nothing less could be expected of him in the failure of that than the immediate contraction of another.

His errand at Barton, in fact, was a simple one. It was only to ask Elinor to marry him; and considering that he was not altogether inexperienced in such a question, it might be strange that he should feel so uncomfortable in the present case as he really did, so much in need of encouragement and fresh air.

—*on Edward Ferrars, in* Sense and Sensibility

* * *

. . . "And how do you think I mean to amuse myself on the days that I do not hunt? I am grown too old to go out more than three times a week; but I have a plan for the intermediate days, and what do you think it is?"

"To walk and ride with me, to be sure."

"Not exactly, though I shall be happy to do both, but *that* would be exercise only to my body, and I must take care of my mind. Besides, *that* would be all recreation and indulgence, without the wholesome alloy of labor, and I do not like to eat the bread of idleness. No, my plan is to make Fanny Price in love with me."

"Fanny Price! Nonsense! No, no. You ought to be satisfied with her two cousins."

"But I cannot be satisfied without Fanny Price, without making a small hole in Fanny Price's heart."

—*Henry Crawford and his sister Mary, in* Mansfield Park

* * *

"Was it unpardonable to think it worth my while to come? And to arrive with some degree of hope? You were single. It was possible that you might retain the feelings of the past, as I did; and one encouragement happened to be mine. I could never doubt that you would be loved and sought by others, but I knew to a certainty that you had refused one man, at least, of better pretensions than myself; and I could not help often saying, 'Was this for me?'"

—*Colonel Wentworth to Anne Elliot, in* Persuasion

* * *

"I lay it down as a general rule, Harriet, that if a woman doubts as to whether she should accept a man or not, she certainly ought to refuse him. If she can hesitate as to 'Yes,' she ought to say 'No' directly. It is not a state to be safely entered into with doubtful feelings, with half a heart. I thought it my duty as a friend, and older than yourself, to say thus much to you. But do not imagine that I want to influence you."

—*Emma Woodhouse to Harriet Smith, regarding Robert Martin's proposal to Harriet, in* Emma

* * *

Do not be in a hurry; depend upon it, the right Man will come at last; you will in the course of the next two or three years, meet with someone more generally unexceptionable than anyone you have yet known, who will love you as warmly as ever *He* did, who will so completely attach you, that you will feel you never really loved before.

—*from a letter to her niece Fanny Knight, 1816*

* * *

Till now that she was threatened with its loss, Emma had never known how much of her happiness depended on

being *first* with Mr. Knightley, first in interest and affection.—Satisfied that it was so, and feeling it her due, she
had enjoyed it without reflection; and only in the dread
of being supplanted, found how inexpressibly important
it had been.

—*on Emma Woodhouse, in* Emma

* * *

She was of course only too good for him; but as nobody
minds having what is too good for them, he was very
steadily earnest in the pursuit of the blessing . . .

—*on Fanny Price and Edmund Bertram, in* Mansfield Park

* * *

LOVE

Much will forever be unknown about Jane Austen's affairs of the heart. Her sister, Cassandra, in whom she confided most, is believed to have destroyed a number of Jane's letters, ones that might reveal more details about the few men who seem to have possibly stolen her heart. One of Jane Austen's romantic attractions was Tom Lefroy, a young man who had traveled to Austen's hometown of Hampshire from Ireland to visit his relations, who were good friends of the Austens' and their closest neighbors. (His aunt, known to their circle as "Madam Lefroy," a great fan of books and reading, was, though of course much older, a close personal friend and something of a literary mentor to the young Jane.)

Jane, who was twenty at the time, wrote to her sister, "I am almost afraid to tell you how my Irish friend and I behaved. Imagine to yourself everything most profligate and shocking in the way of dancing and sitting down together. . . . He is a very gentlemanlike, good-looking, pleasant young man I assure you. But as to our having ever met, except at the three last balls, I cannot say much; for he is so excessively laughed at about me at Ashe, that he is ashamed of coming to Steventon, and ran away when we called on Mrs. Lefroy a few days ago." He had, she writes in her letter, ". . . but *one* fault, which time will, I trust, entirely remove—it is that his morning coat is a great deal too light. He is a very great admirer of Tom Jones and therefore wears the same coloured clothes, I imagine, which *he* did [in the novel by Henry Fielding] when he was wounded." Later, she writes again about a ball to take place before Tom leaves the country: "I rather expect to receive an offer from my friend in the course of the evening. I shall refuse him, however, unless he promises to give away his white Coat."

For all her glib humor about him, Austen seems to have had more than a passing attraction to this apparently shy, good-hearted, and intelligent young man. But a real romance was not to be. Tom was from a large and not wealthy family, and his great-uncle was paying to groom him for a legal career (he eventually became Lord Chief Justice of Ireland), so that he could help to provide for them financially. What happened next is not entirely clear. It seems that Tom's family, worried about the flirtation escalating to an engagement between this young and impoverished pair, sent him off to London soon after, to study there under the watch of his great-uncle, and that he eventually returned to Ireland and married there. It must have been painful for her. Three years later she wrote to her sister that she had spoken to Mrs. Lefroy, who neglected to mention her nephew, and said that she herself had been "too proud to make any enquiries."

There seems to have been another, later affair of the heart in Austen's life. After Jane's death, Cassandra revealed to a number of her nieces and nephews that there had been a certain gentleman whom she and Jane had met on a trip to the seaside, when Jane was somewhere in her mid-to-late twenties. Cassandra had been very impressed with him, and believed Jane to have been too. When they parted from him, after a period of several weeks, he had expressed the intention of seeing Jane again, inquiring where she would be the following summer—Cassandra said that she felt he was quite serious in his desire to pursue her, and likely would have met with success. But Jane took a cruel blow when the gentleman suddenly passed away.

In an odd and tragic parallel, the great love of Cassandra's life, her fiancé, Tom Fowle, had met his own sudden death, when he caught yellow fever while on a trip to the West Indies, a number of years before the sisters' seaside trip. Cassandra had never allowed herself to fall in love again, and perhaps, following her sister's example, neither did Jane.

The enthusiasm of a woman's love is even beyond the biographer's. To her, the [beloved's] handwriting itself, independent of anything it may convey, is a blessedness.

—*from* Mansfield Park

* * *

To be fond of dancing was a certain step towards falling in love; and very lively hopes of Mr. Bingley's heart were entertained.

—*from* Pride and Prejudice

* * *

"There is safety in reserve, but no attraction. One cannot love a reserved person."

"Not till the reserve ceases towards one's self; and then the attraction may be the greater."

—*Frank Churchill and Emma Woodhouse, in* Emma

* * *

Half the sum of attraction, on either side, might have been enough, for he had nothing to do, and she had hardly anybody to love . . .

—*on Captain Wentworth and Anne Elliot, in* Persuasion

* * *

"So, Lizzie," said he one day, "your sister is crossed in love, I find. I congratulate her. Next to being married, a girl likes to be crossed a little in love now and then. It is something to think of, and it gives her a sort of distinction among her companions."

—*Mr. Darcy to Elizabeth Bennet, referring to her sister Jane,*
in Pride and Prejudice

✳　✳　✳

"This man is almost too gallant to be in love," thought Emma.

—*Emma Woodhouse, about Mr. Elton, in* Emma

✳　✳　✳

". . . the more I know of the world the more I am convinced that I shall never see a man whom I can really love. I require so much!"

—*Marianne Dashwood to her mother, in*
Sense and Sensibility

✳　✳　✳

. . . from the time of our being in London together, I thought you really very much in love.—But you certainly are not at all—there is no concealing it.—What strange creatures we are!—It seems as if your being secure of him (as you say yourself) had made you Indifferent.

—*from a letter to her niece Fanny Knight,*
  November 18–20, 1814

* * *

Elizabeth's spirits soon rising to playfulness again, she wanted Mr. Darcy to account for his having ever fallen in love with her. "How could you begin?" she said. "I can comprehend your going on charmingly, when you had once made a beginning; but what could set you off in the first place?"

"I cannot fix on the hour, or the spot, or the look, or the words, which laid the foundation. It is too long ago. I was in the middle before I knew that I *had* begun."

"My beauty you had early withstood, and as for my manners—my behavior to *you* was at least always bordering on uncivil, and I never spoke to you without rather wishing to give you pain than not. Now, be sincere; did you admire me for my impertinence?"

"For the liveliness of your mind, I did."

"You may as well call it impertinence at once. It was very little less. The fact is, that you were sick of civility, of deference, of officious attention. You were disgusted with the women who were always speaking and looking and thinking for your approbation alone. I roused and interested you, because I was so unlike *them*. Had you not been really amiable, you would have hated me for it; but, in spite of the pains you took to disguise yourself, your feelings were always noble and just; and, in your heart, you thoroughly despised the persons who so assiduously courted you. There—I have saved you all the trouble of accounting for it; and really, all things considered, I begin to think it perfectly reasonable. To be sure, you know no actual good of me—but nobody thinks of *that* when they fall in love."

—*Elizabeth Bennet and Mr. Darcy, in* Pride and Prejudice

✳   ✳   ✳

Let no one presume to give the feelings of a young woman on receiving the assurance of that affection of which she has scarcely allowed herself to entertain a hope.

—*on Fanny Price, in love with Edmund Bertram, in*
   Mansfield Park

✳   ✳   ✳

What totally different feelings did Emma take back into the house from what she had brought out!—she had then been only daring to hope for a little respite of suffering;—she was now in an exquisite flutter of happiness, and such happiness moreover as she believed must still be greater when the flutter should have passed away.

They sat down to tea—the same party round the same table—how often it had been collected!—and how often had her eyes fallen on the same shrubs in the lawn, and observed the same beautiful effect of the western sun!—But never in such a state of spirits, never in anything like it; and it was with difficulty that she could summon enough of her usual self to be the attentive lady of the house, or even the attentive daughter.

—*on Emma Woodhouse, after learning of Mr. Knightley's love for her, in* Emma

*   *   *

"What glorious weather for the Admiral and my sister! They meant to take a long drive this morning; perhaps we may hail them from some of these hills. They talked of coming into this side of the country. I wonder whereabouts they will upset today. Oh! it does happen very often I assure you—but my sister makes nothing of it— she would as lieve be tossed out as not."

"Ah, you make the most of it, I know," cried Louisa, "but if it were really so, I should do just the same in her place. If I loved a man as she loves the Admiral, I would be always with him, nothing should ever separate us, and I would rather be overturned by him, than driven safely by anybody else."

It was spoken with enthusiasm.

"Had you?" cried he, catching the same tone; "I honor you!" And there was silence between them for a little while.

—*Captain Wentworth and Louisa Musgrove, in* Persuasion

*   *   *

". . . I am pleased that you have learnt to love a hyacinth. The mere habit of learning to love is the thing; and a teachableness of disposition in a young lady is a great blessing. . . ."

—*Henry Tilney to Catherine Morland, in*
    Northanger Abbey

*   *   *

Fanny's graces of manner and goodness of heart were the exhaustless themes. The gentleness, modesty, and sweetness of her character were warmly expatiated on;

that sweetness which makes so essential a part of every woman's worth in the judgment of man, that though he sometimes loves where it is not, he can never believe it absent.

—*on Henry Crawford's admiration for Fanny Price, in* Mansfield Park

* * *

"If I loved you less, I might be able to talk about it more."

—*Mr. Knightley to Emma Woodhouse, in* Emma

* * *

Colonel Brandon was now as happy as all those who best loved him believed he deserved to be;—in Marianne he was consoled for every past affliction;—her regard and her society restored his mind to animation, and his spirits to cheerfulness; and that Marianne found her own happiness in forming his, was equally the persuasion and delight of each observing friend. Marianne could never love by halves; and her whole heart became, in time, as much devoted to her husband as it had once been to Willoughby.

—*from* Sense and Sensibility

*   *   *

MARRIAGE

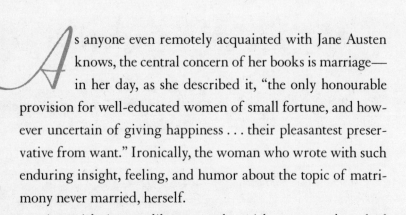

As anyone even remotely acquainted with Jane Austen knows, the central concern of her books is marriage—in her day, as she described it, "the only honourable provision for well-educated women of small fortune, and however uncertain of giving happiness . . . their pleasantest preservative from want." Ironically, the woman who wrote with such enduring insight, feeling, and humor about the topic of matrimony never married, herself.

As a girl, Austen, like most other girls, seems to have had marriage on her mind: she entered herself three separate times in the registry books at Steventon parish, where her father was rector, with three different imaginary husbands. As a young woman, she had a number of suitors and at least two affairs of the heart, but the only proposal we know for sure she received was from a man by the unfortunate name of Harris Bigg-Wither. Jane and her sister, Cassandra, who were good friends with Harris's sisters, visited the family in 1802, when Jane was twenty-seven (in those days, pretty well "over the hill"). Harris, though six years younger than Jane, was heir to an impressive estate, and thus in a position to propose. Probably to her great surprise, he did. Jane, who did not love Harris, accepted his offer. Though we can only imagine the emotional struggle she must have endured—her desire to gain financial security for her family versus the unfortunate truth of her feelings—we do know that the morning after accepting Harris's offer, she promptly rejected it. While there was surely some embarrassment and discomfort on her part (she later wrote in a letter to her niece Fanny Knight, ". . . the unpleasantness of appearing fickle is certainly great . . ."), it was obviously not enough to prevent her from holding to her own passionately held view, expressed many times in both her fiction and her letters, that "nothing can be compared to the misery of being bound *without* love."

While many Austen fans are dismayed to learn that their beloved Jane never got the happy ending that she unfailingly engineered for her heroines, one can only speculate as to whether and how much it pained her. Whatever was in her heart, or in the more personal letters that Cassandra is believed to have systematically destroyed, Austen seemed to cover up in her surviving correspondence by poking fun at herself. And though she often lamented her monetary difficulties ("Single Women," she wrote to Fanny, "have a dreadful propensity for being poor"), by the time of Bigg-Wither's proposal she had already finished three of her novels—all as yet unpublished—and was firmly committed to her chosen path. Had she married Bigg-Wither, become the mistress of his estate, and given birth to a brigade of Bigg-Withers, she certainly could never have had the time to devote herself to her serious literary ambitions, a fact of which she seems to have been well aware.

And maybe it's there that those fans can find some solace. While fate never delivered the ideal that on some level Austen may have hoped for—a man who could offer financial support

to her family and also touch her heart—she did have the joy
and satisfaction of creating worlds of her own, where romances with happy endings were definitely more obliging.

"My being charming, Harriet, is not quite enough to in-
duce me to marry; I must find other people charming—
one other person at least."
   —*Emma Woodhouse to Harriet Smith, in* Emma

*   *   *

When any two people take it into their heads to marry,
they are pretty sure by perseverance to carry their point,
be they ever so poor, or ever so imprudent, or ever so little
likely to be necessary to each other's ultimate comfort.
   —*on Captain Wentworth and Anne Elliot, in* Persuasion

*   *   *

Mr. Rushworth could hardly be more impatient for the
marriage than herself. In all the important preparations

of the mind she was complete; being prepared for matrimony by an hatred of home, restraint, and tranquility; by the misery of disappointed affection, and contempt of the man she was to marry.

—*on Maria Bertram, in* Mansfield Park

* * *

"... it is always incomprehensible to a man that a woman should ever refuse an offer of marriage."

—*Emma Woodhouse to Mr. Knightley, in* Emma

* * *

She had only two daughters, both of whom she had lived to see respectably married, and she now therefore had nothing to do but to marry all the rest of the world.

—*on Mrs. Jennings, in* Sense and Sensibility

* * *

"I wish Jane success with all my heart; and if she were married to him tomorrow, I should think she had as good a chance of happiness as if she were to be studying his character for a twelve-month. Happiness in marriage is entirely a matter of chance. If the dispositions of the parties are ever so well known to each other or ever so similar beforehand, it does not advance their felicity in the least. They always grow sufficiently unlike afterwards to have their share of vexation; and it is better to know as little as possible of the defects of the person with whom you are to pass your life."

—*Charlotte Lucas to Elizabeth Bennet, about Elizabeth's sister Jane and Mr. Bingley, in* Pride and Prejudice

* * *

To begin perfect happiness at the respective ages of twenty-six and eighteen, is to do pretty well . . .

—*on the marriage of Henry Tilney and Catherine Morland, in* Northanger Abbey

* * *

"I am of a cautious temper, and unwilling to risk my happiness in a hurry. Nobody can think more highly of the matrimonial state than myself. I consider the blessing of

a wife as most justly described in those discreet lines of
the poet, 'Heaven's *last* best gift.'"

—*Henry Crawford, quoting Milton's* Paradise Lost *to*
his sister Mary and their half sister, Mrs. Grant, in
Mansfield Park

* * *

"Oh, Mr. Bennet, you are wanted immediately; we are all
in an uproar. You must come and make Lizzy marry Mr.
Collins, for she vows she will not have him, and if you
do not make haste he will change his mind and not have
her." . . .

"I do not have the pleasure of understanding you,"
said he [to Mrs. Bennet], when she had finished her
speech. "Of what are you talking?"

"Of Mr. Collins and Lizzy. Lizzy declares she will
not have Mr. Collins, and Mr. Collins begins to say he
will not have Lizzy." . . .

"Come here, child," cried her father as she appeared.
"I have sent for you on an affair of importance. I understand that Mr. Collins has made you an offer of marriage.

Is it true?" Elizabeth replied that it was. "Very well—and this offer of marriage you have refused?"

"I have, sir."

"Very well. We now come to the point. Your mother insists upon your accepting it. Is it not so, Mrs. Bennet?"

"Yes, or I will never see her again."

"An unhappy alternative is before you, Elizabeth. From this day you must be a stranger to one of your parents.—Your mother will never see you again if you do *not* marry Mr. Collins, and I will never see you again if you *do*."

—*from* Pride and Prejudice

*   *   *

[Miss Bigg] writes me word that Miss Blachford *is* married, but I have never seen it in the Papers. And one may as well be single if the Wedding is not to be in print.

—*from a letter to her niece Anna (Austen) Lefroy, most likely late February—early March, 1815*

*   *   *

"I pay very little regard . . . to what any young person says on the subject of marriage. If they profess a disinclination for it, I only set it down that they have not yet seen the right person."

   —*Mrs. Grant, in* Mansfield Park

* * *

"Human nature is so well-disposed towards those who are in interesting situations, that a young person, who either marries or dies, is sure of being kindly spoken of."

   —*from* Pride and Prejudice

* * *

It would be an excellent match, for *he* was rich, and *she* was handsome.

   —*on Colonel Brandon and Marianne Dashwood, as viewed*
     by Mrs. Jennings, in Sense and Sensibility

* * *

His temper might perhaps be a little soured by finding, like many others of his sex, that through some unaccountable bias in favor of beauty, he was the husband of a very silly woman.

—*on Mr. Palmer and Mrs. Palmer, in* Sense and Sensibility

* * *

"It was a very proper wedding. The bride was elegantly dressed—the two bridesmaids were duly inferior—her father gave her away—her mother stood with salts in her hand, expecting to be agitated—her aunt tried to cry—and the service was impressively read by Dr. Grant. Nothing could be objected to when it came under the discussion of the neighborhood, except that the carriage which conveyed the bride and bridegroom and Julia from the church door to Sotherton, was the same chaise which Mr. Rushworth had used for a twelvemonth before. In everything else the etiquette of the day might stand the strictest investigation."

—*on the wedding of Maria Bertram to Mr. Rushworth, in* Mansfield Park

* * *

"To be so bent on marriage—to pursue a man merely for the sake of situation—is a sort of thing that shocks me; I cannot understand it. Poverty is a great evil, but to a woman of education and feeling it ought not, it cannot be the greatest—I would rather be a teacher at a school (and I can think of nothing worse) than marry a man I did not like."

—*Emma Watson, in* The Watsons (*an unfinished novel, circa 1803–1805*)

*   *   *

"I had not known you a month before I felt that you were the last man in the world whom I could ever be prevailed on to marry."

—*Elizabeth Bennet to Mr. Darcy, in* Pride and Prejudice

*   *   *

". . . Everybody is taken in at some period or other."

"Not always in marriage, dear Mary."

"In marriage especially. With all due respect to such of the present company as chance to be married, my dear Mrs. Grant, there is not one in a hundred of either sex, who is not taken in when they marry. Look where I will, I see that it *is* so; and I feel that it *must* be so when I consider that it is, of all transactions, the one in which people expect the most from others, and are the least honest themselves."

—*Mary Crawford and her half sister, Mrs. Grant, in*
   Mansfield Park

*   *   *

Marianne Dashwood was born to an extraordinary fate. She was born to discover the falsehood of her own opinions, and to counteract, by her conduct, her most favorite maxims. She was born to overcome an affection formed so late in life as at seventeen, and with no sentiment superior to strong esteem and lively friendship, voluntarily to give her hand to another!—and *that* other, a man who had suffered no less than herself under the event of a former attachment, whom two years before, she had considered too old to be married,—and who still sought the constitutional safeguard of a flannel waistcoat!

But so it was. Instead of falling a sacrifice to an irresistible passion, as once she had fondly flattered herself with expecting,—instead of remaining even forever with her mother, and finding her only pleasures in retirement and study, as afterwards in her more calm and sober judgment she had determined on,—she found herself at nineteen submitting to new attachments, entering on new duties, placed in a new home, a wife, the mistress of a family, and the patroness of a village.

—*on Marianne Dashwood and Colonel Brandon, in*
Sense and Sensibility

* * *

It is a truth universally acknowledged, that a single man in possession of a good fortune must be in want of a wife.

However little known the views of such a man may be on his first entering a neighborhood, this truth is so well fixed in the minds of the surrounding families, that he is considered as the rightful property of some one or other of their daughters.

—*from* Pride and Prejudice

* * *

I consider everybody as having the right to marry *once* in their Lives for Love, if they can . . .
   —*from a letter to her sister, Cassandra,*
      December 27–28, 1808

* * *

MONEY

Money is a matter of huge consequence to nearly all of Jane Austen's heroines—as it was to Austen herself. In the late eighteenth and early nineteenth centuries, it wasn't respectable for women of Austen's social class to go out to work, even as teachers or governesses. While some were forced by circumstances to do so, they were considered a social disgrace. Following the tradition of primogeniture, women could not inherit land. To keep estates from being broken up (and, obviously, to keep the power in the hands of men), land passed from eldest son to eldest son—or, if there was no son, the estate could be entailed to another male relation (as is the case with the Bennets' home in *Pride and Prejudice*, which

Mr. Collins stands to inherit). So if a woman wasn't lucky enough to inherit cash, her only recourse was to try to marry her way into it. This could be especially tricky for a woman from a poor family, since eligible men without a large chunk of change of their own often had to marry "up"—that is, wed a woman with a hefty dowry—as they frequently were called upon to support their younger brothers and sisters along with any children they might produce themselves. A woman's predicament became especially dire if her family (again, like the Bennets) depended on her marrying well to guarantee their financial security along with her own. For such a woman, and there were many in Austen's day, seeking a husband, aside from any desire for romance, love, or companionship, was a serious and very practical economic affair—one in which parents, relations, and friends usually stuck their noses, whether they were asked to or not.

Austen's own family was far from destitute, but certainly not rich. Her father, the Reverend George Austen, and her mother, Cassandra Leigh Austen, were members of the lower end of the gentry—that is, they owned land and had a certain degree of social status—but they both came from the poorer branches of their families, and were able to marry only because of the generosity of their wealthier relations. The Reverend and Mrs. Austen managed to support Jane and her slew of siblings in a simple but fairly comfortable style at the Steventon Rectory, in Hampshire, where the family lived for many years (later moving to Bath—a hard blow to Jane, who was quite attached to her childhood home), by supplementing the reverend's income as rector and the food produced by their small family farm with money earned by housing and tutoring young male students. (Jane and her sister, Cassandra, were sent away briefly to be tutored themselves in 1783, to Oxford and then Southampton, but returned home after they caught typhus from troops stationed there; they also attended the Abbey House School in Reading for almost two years, but the tuition proved too great to be afforded, and they received the rest of their education at home.) As neither Jane nor her sister ever married, their father, while he lived, had to provide for all of their financial support. Jane had published only one novel up to that point, and, though she did earn some money from her writing during her lifetime, it was a shockingly small amount given the degree of her later literary success.

After her father's sudden death in 1805 (when Jane was thirty), she, Cassandra, and their mother had to rely almost completely on her brothers for support. They first went to live with her brother Frank (Francis) and his wife and daughters in Southampton. Four years later, they moved to her brother Edward's estate, Chawton, back in Jane's beloved Hampshire. During these years, they lived on an extremely small income, an amount generally considered barely enough to support a single woman of their social class. Jane did receive some sort of regular stipend from Mrs. Knight, the adopted mother of her brother Edward (the Knights, distant cousins of the Austens, had no children, and chose Edward as their heir); she refers to a letter containing Mrs. Knight's "usual Fee" in 1808. Still, money seems always to have been tight—much appreciated when it was plentiful enough, and much lamented when it was not. "I have now therefore written myself into £250," she wrote to her brother Frank, "—which only makes me long for more." Her characters frequently reflect much the same sentiment.

". . . a very narrow income has a tendency to contract the mind, and sour the temper."

　—*Emma Woodhouse to Harriet Smith, in* Emma

*　*　*

I am tolerably glad to hear that Edward's [their brother's] income is so good a one—as glad as I can at anybody's being rich besides You & me . . .

　—*from a letter to her sister, Cassandra, January 8–9, 1799*

*　*　*

"If you observe, people always live forever when there is any annuity to be paid them."

　—*Fanny Dashwood to her husband, John, in*
　　Sense and Sensibility

*　*　*

"Be honest and poor, by all means—but I shall not envy you; I do not much think I will even respect you. I have a much greater respect for those that are honest and rich."

　—*Mary Crawford to Edmund Bertram, in* Mansfield Park

* * *

Thank you—but it is not settled yet whether I *do* hazard
a 2^d Edition. . . . People are more ready to borrow &
praise, than to buy—which I cannot wonder at;—but
tho' I like praise as well as anybody, I like what Edward
[one of her older brothers] calls *Pewter* too.

   —*from a letter to her niece Fanny Knight,*

     November 30, 1814

* * *

Miss Crawford, who had been repeatedly eyeing Dr.
Grant and Edmund, now observed, "Those gentlemen
must have some very interesting points to discuss."

   "The most interesting in the world," replied her
brother—"how to make money—how to turn a good income into a better. Dr. Grant is giving Bertram instructions
about the living he is to step into so soon. . . . I am glad
Bertram will be so well off. He will have a very pretty income to make ducks and drakes with, and earned without
much trouble. I apprehend he will not have less than seven

hundred a year. Seven hundred a year is a fine thing for a younger brother; and as of course he will still live at home, it will all be for his *menus plaisirs* [little luxuries] . . ."

His sister tried to laugh off her feelings by saying, "Nothing amuses me more than the easy manner which with everybody settles the abundance of those who have a great deal less than themselves. You would look rather blank, Henry, if your *menus plaisirs* were to be limited to seven hundred a year."

—*Mary Crawford to her brother Henry, in* Mansfield Park

* * *

"But still, you will be an old maid! And that's so dreadful!"

"Never mind, Harriet, I shall not be a poor old maid; and it is poverty only which makes celibacy contemptible to a generous public! A single woman, with a very narrow income, must be a ridiculous, disagreeable, old maid! the proper sport of boys and girls; but a single woman, of good fortune, is always respectable, and may be as sensible and pleasant as anybody else."

—*Harriet Smith and Emma Woodhouse, in* Emma

* * *

People get so horribly poor & economical in this part of the World, that I have no patience with them.—Kent is the only place for happiness, Everybody is rich there.

—*from a letter to her sister, Cassandra, December 18–19, 1798*

* * *

"My notion of things is simple enough. Let me only have the girl I like, say I, with a comfortable house over my head, and what care I for all the rest? Fortune is nothing. I am sure of a good income of my own; and if she had not a penny, why so much the better."

"Very true. I think like you there. If there is a good fortune on one side, there can be no occasion for any on the other. No matter which has it, so that there is enough. I hate the idea of one great fortune looking out for another."

—*Henry Tilney and Catherine Morland, in*
  Northanger Abbey

* * *

"Pray, my dear aunt, what is the difference in matrimonial affairs, between the mercenary and the prudent motive? Where does discretion end, and avarice begin?"

—*Elizabeth Bennet to her aunt, Mrs. Gardiner, in*
Pride and Prejudice

* * *

"What have wealth or grandeur to do with happiness?"

"Grandeur has but little," said Elinor, "but wealth has much to do with it."

"Elinor, for shame!" said Marianne. "Money can only give happiness where there is nothing else to give it . . ."

—*Marianne Dashwood and her sister Elinor, in*
Sense and Sensibility

* * *

". . . after all that romancers may say, there is no doing without money."

—*Isabella Thorpe to Catherine Morland, in*
Northanger Abbey

✳ ✳ ✳

"I do not know anybody who seems more to enjoy the power of doing what he likes than Mr. Darcy."

"He likes to have his own way very well," replied Colonel Fitzwilliam. "But so we all do. It is only that he has better means of having it than many others, because he is rich, and many others are poor. I speak feelingly. A younger son, you know, must be inured to self-denial and dependence."

"In my opinion, the younger son of an Earl can know very little of either. Now, seriously, what have you ever known of self-denial and dependence? When have you been prevented by want of money from going wherever you chose, or procuring anything you had a fancy for?"

"These are home questions—and perhaps I cannot say that I have experienced many hardships of that nature. But in matters of greater weight, I may suffer from the want of money. Younger sons cannot marry where they like."

"Unless where they like women of fortune, which I think they very often do."

　　—*Elizabeth Bennet and Colonel Fitzwilliam, in*
　　　Pride and Prejudice

∗　　∗　　∗

"A large income is the best recipe for happiness I ever heard of. It certainly may secure the myrtle and turkey part of it."

　　—*Mary Crawford, in* Mansfield Park

∗　　∗　　∗

LETTERS AND
LETTER WRITING

Fortunately for those who can't be satisfied with an author's work, but must also know about her life, Jane Austen was a prolific writer of letters. Though she probably wrote many hundreds of letters during her lifetime, to family members and friends, and later to her contacts in the publishing world and the handful of her fans who actually knew who she was (see "Her Own Writing"), only about 150 have survived. Though mostly full of the fairly mundane ups and downs of daily life, the letters give an extremely personal glimpse into Jane Austen's world: meals, housekeeping and other domestic details, family illnesses, births, marriages, and deaths, social calls and "stupid balls" (as Jane was fond of calling them), and so on.

Letters appear often in Austen's books, too, because they were such an essential part of life, but for another reason as well. One of the early forms of novel-writing popular in the 1700s, invented by Samuel Richardson, one of Austen's favorite writers, was the epistolary novel, or novel written entirely in letters—a form that the young Jane tried her hand at a number of times, both in her juvenilia and in early versions of two of her major works. The important innovation that the epistolary novel brought to the development of the literary genre was a focus on the characters' thoughts and feelings. Letters, Richardson discovered, were a handy way to convey both. Both *Sense and Sensibility* (originally titled *Elinor and Marianne*) and *Pride and Prejudice* (originally titled *First Impressions*) began as epistolary novels, and it's interesting to note that Austen, while she did not retain the form, did to some extent retain the use of letters in those novels, especially *Pride and Prejudice*, which contains a great number of them.

Like everything else that passed between men and women in Austen's days, letter writing had its own set of rules. Correspondence between unmarried men and women of marriageable age, who were not related, was considered highly improper—in fact, if such correspondence was discovered, it was tantamount to an engagement announcement, whether intended or not. This may explain why in Jane Austen's plots, certain characters have to rely on other characters to convey certain messages for them, and why others might be so intent on picking up their own mail.

Your letter is come; it came indeed twelve lines ago, but I could not stop to acknowledge it before, & I am glad it did not arrive till I had completed my first sentence, because the sentence had been made ever since yesterday, & I think forms a very good beginning.

—*from a letter to her sister, Cassandra, November 1, 1800*
(Note: Austen's first sentence of that letter is as follows:
"You have written I am sure, tho' I have received no letter from you since your leaving London; —the Post, & not yourself must have been unpunctual.")

* * *

"I knew," said he, "that what I wrote must give you pain, but it was necessary. I hope you have destroyed the letter.

There was one part, especially the opening of it, which I should dread your having the power of reading again. I can remember some expressions which might justly make you hate me. . . . When I wrote that letter . . . I believed myself perfectly calm and cool, but I am since convinced that it was written in a dreadful bitterness of spirit."

"The letter, perhaps, began in bitterness, but it did not end so. The adieu is charity itself."

—*Mr. Darcy and Elizabeth Bennet, in* Pride and Prejudice

* * *

Sir Tho: Miller is dead. I treat you with a dead Baronet in almost every Letter.

—*from a letter to her sister, Cassandra, September 8–9, 1816*

* * *

. . . she seized the scrap of paper on which Edmund had begun writing to her, as a treasure beyond all her hopes, and reading with the tenderest emotion these words, "My very dear Fanny, you must do me the favor to accept—" locked it up with the chain, as the dearest part of the gift. It was the only thing approaching to a letter which she had ever received from him; she might never receive another . . .

—on Fanny Price's feelings for Edmund Bertram, in
   Mansfield Park

* * *

"The post-office has a great charm at one period of our lives. When you have lived to my age, you will begin to think letters are never worth going through the rain for."

There was a little blush, and then this answer, "I must not hope to be ever situated as you are, in the midst of every dearest connection, and therefore I cannot expect that simply growing older should make me indifferent about letters."

"Indifferent! Oh! no—I never conceived you could become indifferent. Letters are no matter of indifference; they are generally a very positive curse."

"You are speaking of letters of business; mine are letters of friendship."

"I have often thought them the worst of the two," replied he coolly. "Business, you know, may bring money, but friendship hardly ever does."

— *Mr. John Knightley and Jane Fairfax, in* Emma

* * *

You have never thanked me for my last Letter, which went by the Cheese.

— *from a letter to her nephew James Edward Austen, July 9, 1816*

* * *

The only pain was in leaving her father, who would certainly miss her, and who, when it came to the point, so little liked her going that he told her to write to him, and almost promised to answer her letter.

— *on Elizabeth and Mr. Bennet, in* Pride and Prejudice

* * *

I wish you Joy of your Birthday twenty times over. —I *shall* be able to send this to the post to day, which exalts me to the utmost pinnacle of human felicity, & makes me bask in the sunshine of Prosperity, or gives me any other sensation of pleasure in studied Language which You may prefer.— Do not be angry with me for not filling my Sheet.

—*from a letter to her sister, Cassandra, January 8–9, 1799*

* * *

"What strange creatures brothers are! You would not write to each other but upon the most urgent necessity in the world; and when obliged to take up the pen to say that such a horse is ill, or such a relation dead, it is done in the fewest possible words. You have but one style among you."

—*Mary Crawford to Edmund Bertram, in* Mansfield Park

* * *

You must read your letters over *five* times in future before you send them, & then perhaps you may find them as entertaining as I do.

—*from a letter to her sister, Cassandra, January 8–9, 1799*

* * *

Expect a most agreeable Letter; for not being over-burdened with subject—(having nothing at all to say)—I shall have no check to my Genius from beginning to end.

—*from a letter to her sister, Cassandra,*

January 21–22, 1801

* * *

"I have nearly determined on explaining myself [his wish to marry Mary Crawford] by letter. To be at an early certainty is a material object. My present state is miserably irksome. Considering everything, I think a letter will be decidedly the best method of explanation. I shall be able to write much that I could not say, and shall be giving her time for reflection before she resolves on her answer, and I am less afraid of the result of reflection than of an immediate hasty impulse; I think I am. My greatest danger would lie in her consulting Mrs. Fraser, and I at a distance unable to help my own cause. A letter exposes to all the evil of consultation, and where the mind is anything short of perfect decision, an adviser may, in an unlucky moment, lead it to do what it may afterwards regret."

—*Edmund Bertram, in a letter to Fanny Price, in*
    Mansfield Park

✳   ✳   ✳

I assure you I am as tired of writing long letters as you can be. What a pity that one should still be so fond of receiving them!—Fanny Austen's Match is quite news, & I am sorry she has behaved so ill. There is some comfort to *us* in her misconduct, that we have not a congratulatory Letter to write.

—*from a letter to her sister, Cassandra, June 30–*
    July 1, 1808

✳   ✳   ✳

You deserve a longer letter than this; but it is my unhappy fate seldom to treat people so well as they deserve.

—*from a letter to her sister, Cassandra,*
    December 24–26, 1798

* * *

I have this moment seen Mrs Driver driven up to the Kitchen Door. I cannot close with a grander circumstance or greater wit—Yrs affec:^ly J.A.

—*from a letter to her sister, Cassandra,*
  September 23–24, 1813

* * *

BOOKS AND READING

*J*ane Austen, an avid reader born into a family of book lovers, must have consumed literature from an early age—from the classics contained in her father's well-stocked library, such as those by Milton and Shakespeare, to the popular Gothic romances and "sentimental novels" of her day, such as those by Ann Radcliffe, to the more realistic, relationship-oriented novels of writers like Fanny Burney and Samuel Richardson. Austen adored the poet William Cowper, whose writing is alluded to in several of her novels, and the moralist writer Dr. Samuel Johnson. She also loved the work of a poet named George Crabbe—a realist, but with humor, much like Jane herself—and there was a running joke in her family about her marrying him. ("No; I have never seen the death of Mrs. Crabbe," she writes in October 1813 to her sister, Cassandra, who apparently had read about it in the papers. "Poor woman! I will comfort *him* as well as I can, but I do not undertake to be good to her children. She had better not leave any.")

Novels may have been Austen's favorite form, to read as well as to write; they are, she states in her famous "aside" in defense of them in *Northanger Abbey,* "work[s] in which the greatest powers of the mind are displayed, in which the most thorough knowledge of human nature, the happiest delineation of its varieties, the liveliest effusions of wit and humour are conveyed to the world in the best chosen language." To understand the zealousness of this defense, one has to realize that novels were, in Austen's day, still a very new form of literature, and an often maligned one. As she notes to Cassandra, in one of her letters, the Austens "[were] great Novel-readers & not ashamed of being so"—indicating that, apparently, many people *were.* Novels, in those days, were viewed negatively on many levels: being works of the imagination that were presented in a sort of guise of reality (rather than factual accounts, such as appeared in newspapers, or theatrical plays, which were obviously not "real"), they were automatically viewed with suspicion—the imagination being regarded, as it was at the time, as rather a dangerous, unpredictable commodity, capable of inciting all manner of trouble, including political revolt— which England had recently endured. Is it any wonder Jane climbed on her soapbox when she set out to revise what was then called *Susan* into *Northanger Abbey*?

Northanger Abbey represents both Austen's love of the literary form of the novel and her derision for the literary conventions that had at that time taken such hold of it. Stock heroines who were sickly sweet models of purity and innocence (or "pictures of perfection" as she referred to them in one of her letters), the improbable appearance of long-lost relatives, overblown emotions such as swooning and fainting, and so on, exasperated her—but, luckily for her readers, drove her to lampoon them, too, first in her juvenilia and then fullscale in *Northanger Abbey*, a novel that is all about novelreaders (both its heroine and its hero are self-proclaimed fans). Catherine Morland (said heroine), who departs, quite pointedly and humorously, from these stock heroines whom Austen abhors in every way, is herself obsessed with all the conventions of the Gothic romances she's devoured. When she gets invited to a real abbey, her desire for shadows, gloom, mystery, secrets, and even murder cause her both terror and mortification, until she finally learns the error of her ways, and, in the light of day, sees Reality as it truly is—which, in Austen's view, is not a bad thing at all.

"But you never read novels, I dare say?"

"Why not?"

"Because they are not clever enough for you— gentlemen read better books."

"The person, be it gentleman or lady, who has not pleasure in a good novel, must be intolerably stupid."

—*Henry Tilney to Catherine Morland, in*
Northanger Abbey

* * *

I have received a very civil note from Mrs Martin requesting my name as a Subscriber to her Library which opens the 14th of January, & my name, or rather Yours is accordingly given. . . . As an inducement to subscribe Mrs Martin tells me that her Collection is not to consist only of Novels, but of every kind of Literature &c &c. She might have spared this pretension to *our* family, who are great Novel-readers & not ashamed of being so;—but it was necessary, I suppose to the self-consequence of half her Subscribers.

—from a letter to her sister, Cassandra, December 18, 1798

* * *

Devereux Forester's being ruined by his Vanity is extremely good; but I wish you would not let him plunge into a "vortex of Dissipation". I do not object to the Thing, but I cannot bear the expression;—it is such thorough novel slang—and so old, that I dare say Adam met with it in the first novel he opened.

—from a letter to her niece Anna Austen (later Lefroy), about
a novel Anna was writing, September 28, 1814

* * *

"I see what you think of me," he said gravely— "I shall make but a poor figure in your journal tomorrow."

"My journal!"

"Yes, I know exactly what you will say: Friday, went to the Lower Rooms; wore my sprigged muslin robe with blue trimmings—plain black shoes—appeared to much advantage; but was strangely harassed by a queer, half-witted man, who would make me dance with him, and distressed me by his nonsense."

"Indeed I shall say no such thing."

"Shall I tell you what you ought to say?"

"If you please."

"I danced with a very agreeable young man, introduced by Mr King; had a great deal of conversation with him—seems a most extraordinary genius—hope I may know more of him. That, madam, is what I *wish* you to say."

"But, perhaps, I keep no journal."

"Perhaps you are not sitting in this room, and I am not sitting by you. These are points in which a doubt is equally possible. Not keep a journal! How are your absent cousins to understand the tenor of your life in Bath without one? How are the civilities and compliments of every day to be related as they ought to be, unless noted down every evening in a journal? How are your various dresses to be remembered, and the particular state of your complexion, and the curl of your hair to be described in all their diversities, without having constant recourse to a journal?—My dear madam, I am not so ignorant of young ladies' ways as you wish to believe me; it is this delightful habit of journalizing which largely contributes to the easy style of writing for which ladies are so generally celebrated. Everybody allows that the talent of writing letters is particularly female. Nature may have done something, but I am sure it must be essentially assisted by the practices of keeping a journal."

—*Henry Tilney and Catherine Morland, in*
    Northanger Abbey

∗   ∗   ∗

She saw no reason against their being happy. . . . He would gain cheerfulness and she would learn to be an enthusiast for [Sir Walter] Scott and Lord Byron; nay, that was probably learned already; of course they had fallen in love over poetry. The idea of Louisa Musgrove turned into a person of literary taste, and sentimental reflection, was amusing, but she had no doubt of it being so.

—*on Anne Elliot discovering the love between Captain Benwick and Louisa Musgrove, in* Persuasion

* * *

Provided that nothing like useful knowledge could be gained by them, provided they were all story and no reflection, she never had any objection to books at all.

—*on Catherine Morland, in* Northanger Abbey

* * *

"I wish," said Margaret, striking out a novel thought, "that somebody would give us all a large fortune apiece!"

"Oh, that they would!" cried Marianne . . .

[. . .] "What magnificent orders would travel from this family to London," said Edward, "in such an event!

What a happy day for booksellers . . . Thomson, Cowper, Scott—[Marianne] would buy them all over and over again; she would buy up every copy, I believe, to prevent their falling into unworthy hands; and she would have every book that tells her how to admire an old twisted tree. Should you not Marianne? . . ."

—*Margaret and Marianne Dashwood, and Edward Ferrars,*
   in Sense and Sensibility

* * *

The progress of the friendship between Catherine and Isabella was quick as its beginning had been warm . . . They called each other by their Christian name, were always arm in arm when they walked, pinned up each other's train for the dance, and were not to be divided in the set; and if a rainy morning deprived them of other enjoyments, they were still resolute in meeting in defiance of wet and dirt, and shut themselves up, to read novels together. Yes, novels;—for I will not adopt that ungenerous and impolitic custom with novel writers, of degrading by their contemptuous censure the

very performances, to the number of which they themselves are adding—joining with their greatest enemies
in bestowing the harshest epithets on such works, and
scarcely ever permitting them to be read by their own
heroine, who, if she accidentally take up a novel, is
sure to turn over its insipid pages with disgust. Alas! If
the heroine of one novel be not patronized by the
heroine of another, from whom can she expect protec-
tion and regard? I cannot approve of it. Let us leave
it to the Reviewers to abuse such effusions of fancy at
their leisure, and over every new novel to talk in
threadbare strains of the trash with which the press
now groans. Let us not desert one another; we are an
injured body. Although our productions have afforded
more extensive and unaffected pleasure than those of
any other literary corporation in the world, no species
of composition has been so much decried. From pride,
ignorance, or fashion, our foes are almost as many as
our readers . . . "I am no novel reader—I seldom look
into novels—Do not imagine that I often read
novels—It is really very well for a novel"—Such is the

common cant. "And what are you reading, Miss?" "Oh! It is only a novel!" replies the young lady; while she lays down her book with affected indifference or momentary shame.—"It is only Cecelia, or Camilla, or Belinda;" or, in short, only some work in which the greatest powers of the mind are displayed, in which the most thorough knowledge of human nature, the happiest delineation of its varieties, the liveliest effusions of wit and humour are conveyed to the world in the best chosen language.

—*from* Northanger Abbey

* * *

. . . he showed himself so intimately acquainted with all the tenderest songs of the one poet, and all the impassioned descriptions of hopeless agony of the other; he repeated, with such tremulous feeling, the various lines which imaged a broken heart, or a mind destroyed by wretchedness, and looked so entirely as if he meant to be understood, that she ventured to hope he did not always read only poetry, and to say that she thought it was the misfortune of poetry to be seldom safely enjoyed by those who enjoyed it completely; and that the strong feelings which alone could estimate it truly, were the very feelings which ought to taste it but sparingly.

—*on Captain Benwick and Anne Elliot, in* Persuasion

* * *

Catherine . . . ventured at last to vary the subject by a question which had long been uppermost in her thoughts; it was, "Have you ever read Udolpho, Mr. Thorpe?"

"Udolpho! Oh, Lord! not I; I never read novels. I have something else to do."

Catherine, humbled and ashamed, was going to apologize for her question, but he prevented her by saying, "Novels are all so full of nonsense and stuff; there has not been a tolerably decent one come out since Tom Jones, except the Monk; I read that t'other day; but as for all the others, they are the stupidest things in creation."

"I think you must like Udolpho, if you were to read it; it is so very interesting."

"Not I, faith! No, if I read any, it shall be Mrs. Radcliffe's; her novels are amusing enough; they are worth reading; some fun and nature in *them.*"

"Udolpho was written by Mrs. Radcliffe," said Catherine, with some hesitation, from the fear of mortifying him.

"No sure; was it? Aye, I remember, so it was; I was thinking of that other stupid book, written by that woman they make such a fuss about, she who married the French emigrant."

"I suppose you mean Camilla?"

"Yes, that's the book: such unnatural stuff!—An old man playing at see-saw! I took up the first volume once and looked it over, but I soon found it would not do; indeed I guessed what sort of stuff it must be before I saw it: as soon as I heard she had married an emigrant, I was sure I should never be able to get through it."

"I have never read it."

"You had no loss I assure you: it is the horridest nonsense you can imagine; there is nothing in the world in it but an old man's playing at see-saw and learning Latin, upon my soul there is not."

—*Catherine Morland and John Thorpe, in*
Northanger Abbey

✳　✳　✳

"Oh! mama, how spiritless, how tame, was Edward's manner in reading to us last night! I felt for my sister most severely. Yet she bore it with such composure she scarcely seemed to notice it. I could hardly keep my seat. To hear those beautiful lines which have frequently driven me almost wild, pronounced with such impenetrable calmness, such dreadful indifference!—"

"He would certainly have done more justice to simple and elegant prose. I thought so at the time, but you *would* give him Cowper."

"Nay, Mama, if he is not to be animated by Cowper!— but we must allow for a difference of taste. Elinor has not my feelings, and therefore she may overlook it, and be happy with him. But it would have broke *my* heart, had I loved him, to hear him read with so little sensibility."

—*Marianne Dashwood to her mother, about her sister Elinor and Edward Ferrars, in* Sense and Sensibility

*   *   *

Because they were fond of reading, she fancied them satirical: perhaps without exactly knowing what it was to be satirical; but that did not signify.

—*on Lady Middleton, regarding Elinor and Marianne Dashwood, in* Sense and Sensibility

*   *   *

"You are fond of history!—and so are Mr. Allen and my father; and I have two brothers who do not dislike it. So many instances within my small circle of friends is remarkable! At this rate, I shall not pity the writers of history any longer. If people like to read their books, it is all very well, but to be at so much trouble in filling great volumes, which, as I used to think, nobody would willingly ever look into, to be laboring only for the torment of little boys and girls, always struck me as a hard fate."

—*Catherine Morland, on the subject of history books, in*
Northanger Abbey

* * *

"Shakespeare one gets acquainted with without knowing how. It is part of an Englishman's constitution. His thoughts and beauties are so spread abroad that one touches them everywhere; one is intimate with him by instinct."

—*Henry Crawford, in* Mansfield Park

* * *

"Well, Marianne," said Elinor, as soon as he had left them, "for one morning I think you have done pretty well. You have already ascertained Mr. Willoughby's opinion in almost every matter of importance. You know what he thinks of Cowper and Scott; you are certain of his estimating their beauties as he ought, and you have received every assurance of his admiring Pope no more than is proper. But how is your acquaintance to be long supported, under such extraordinary dispatch of every subject for discourse? You will soon have exhausted each favorite topic. Another meeting will suffice to explain his sentiments on picturesque beauty, and second marriages, and then you can have nothing further to ask."

—*Elinor Dashwood to her sister Marianne, in*
    Sense and Sensibility

* * *

But from fifteen to seventeen she was in training for a heroine; she read all such works as heroines must read to supply their memories with those quotations which are so serviceable and so soothing in the vicissitudes of their eventful lives . . .

—*on Catherine Morland, in* Northanger Abbey

* * *

HER OWN WRITING

W hat would Jane Austen think if she could see her ongoing wild success, and the enthusiasm of her countless readers and admirers around the world today? Austen's six major novels have been translated into at least thirty-five languages, and have never been out of print. And then there are the films, Broadway shows, TV miniseries, sequels, and other adaptations and permutations (not to mention Ph.D. dissertations). It's difficult to believe she never earned enough from her writing to support herself, and most of her reading public, during her life, never even knew her name.

Sense and Sensibility, Austen's first published work (though not the first of her major novels to be written), released in 1811, contained a title page stating that it was "By a Lady." Her next book, *Pride and Prejudice,* published in 1813, was credited to "The Author of Sense and Sensibility"—with *Mansfield Park* (1814) and then *Emma* (1815) following in the same manner. It was not until after her death, in 1817, through her obituaries, and then the following year, through the joint publication of *Northanger Abbey* and *Persuasion* (which included both her name and her brother Henry's "Biographical Notice of the Author"), that Austen was officially "outed"—though Henry had begun, against her wishes, to reveal the "Secret" of her authorship as early as 1813, as she mentions in a letter to her brother Frank. While her dismay, in that letter, about being exposed may seem like sarcasm or false humility to the casual reader, it was anything but. Women of Austen's class (though her family was monetarily poor, they were still considered, socially, gentry—that is, they owned land and mingled with well-to-do sorts) were not supposed to write, at least not for money, because, despite the fact that such women often had to *marry* for money, they were not supposed to *need* it.

Austen not only needed the income, she liked earning it, too. She was proud of her books, as her letters show, and proud of the money they made her—pittance that it was, all things considered. Which leads Austen fans to ponder the question: Why, for nearly ten years of her life, roughly between the ages of twenty-five and thirty-five, did Austen, always so prolific otherwise, produce no work? There is little hard evidence to explain this "fallow period." To the torment of Janeites everywhere, there is also very little correspondence from certain stretches of this period, and if any explanation for her lack of creative output was written to her sister, Cassandra (or anyone else), it must have been destroyed. Speculations have run rampant: Among the most popular are that a) Austen was too depressed over her family's move from Steventon to Bath to write; b) her established writing routine was disrupted by the move, and subsequent moves thereafter; c) she was busy kicking up her heels and enjoying life far too much to write; and d) she was too depressed over the death of the "mysterious gentleman" (see the chapter "Love"). Whatever the reason, it seems to have been, in the eyes of Cassandra, at least, a subject not fitting for a Lady to reveal.

I begin already to weigh my words & sentences more than I did, & am looking about for a sentiment, an illustration or a metaphor in every corner of the room. Could my Ideas flow as fast as the rain in the Storecloset, it would be charming.

  —*from a letter to her sister, Cassandra, January 24, 1809*

     *   *   *

No, indeed, I am never too busy to think of S&S [*Sense and Sensibility*]. I can no more forget it, than a mother can forget her sucking child; & I am much obliged to you for your enquiries.

  —*from a letter to her sister, Cassandra, April 25, 1811*

     *   *   *

We have tried to get Self-controul [a popular novel of the time, by Mary Brunton], but in vain. I *should* like to know what her Estimate is—but am always half afraid of finding a clever novel *too clever*—and of finding my own story & my own people all forestalled.

—*from a letter to her sister, Cassandra, April 30, 1811*

(*Note: Austen apparently got hold of a copy of the book, as on October 11–12, 1813, she wrote to her sister, Cassandra, with tongue characteristically in cheek:*)

I am looking over Self Control again, & my opinion is confirmed of its' being an excellently-meant, elegantly-written Work, without anything of Nature or Probability in it. I declare I do not know whether Laura's passage down the American River is not the most natural, possible, every-day thing she ever does.

(*And, on November 24, 1814, she wrote to her niece Anna Austen that she would write as close an imitation of it as she could, but that:*)

—I will improve upon it; —my Heroine shall not merely be wafted down an American river in a boat by herself,

she shall cross the Atlantic in the same way & never stop
till she reaches Gravesent.

*　　*　　*

. . . the truth is that the Secret has spread so far as to
be scarcely the shadow of a Secret now—& that I
beleive whenever the 3ᵈ appears, I shall not even at-
tempt to tell Lies about it. People shall pay for their
Knowledge if I can make them.—Henry heard P. & P.
[*Pride and Prejudice*] warmly praised in Scotland . . .
& what does he do in the warmth of his Brotherly vanity and Love, but immediately tell them who wrote
it!—A Thing once set going in that way—one knows
how it spreads!—and he, dear Creature, has set it
going so much more than once. I know it is all done
from affection & partiality . . . I am trying to harden
myself.

　　—*from a letter to her brother Francis, on the "Secret" of her*
　　　authorship, September 25, 1813

*　　*　　*

I want to tell you that I have got my own darling Child
[her first published copy of *Pride and Prejudice*] from
London.

   —from a letter to her sister, Cassandra, January 29, 1813

✳   ✳   ✳

I must confess that *I* think her as delightful a creature as
ever appeared in print, & how I shall be able to tolerate
those who do not like *her* at least, I do not know.

   —on Elizabeth Bennet, in a letter to her sister, Cassandra,
     January 29, 1813

✳   ✳   ✳

The work is rather too light & bright & sparkling;—it
wants shade;—it wants to be stretched out here & there
with a long Chapter—of sense if it could be had, if not
of solemn specious nonsense—about something uncon-
nected with the story; an Essay on Writing, a critique
on Walter Scott, or the history of Buonaparte—or anything that would form a contrast & bring the reader
with increased delight to the playful & Epigrammatism

of the general stile.—I doubt your quite agreeing with me here. I know your starched Notions.

—*on* Pride and Prejudice, *from a letter to her sister,*
Cassandra, February 4, 1813

* * *

I dined upon Goose yesterday—which I hope will secure a good Sale of my 2^d Edition [of *Sense and Sensibility*].

—*from a letter to her sister, Cassandra, October 11–12,*
1813

* * *

Since I wrote last, my 2^d Edit. [of *Sense and Sensibility*] has stared me in the face. . . . I cannot help hoping that *many* will feel themselves obliged to buy it. I shall not mind imagining it a disagreeable Duty to them, so as they do it.

—*from a letter to her sister, Cassandra, November 6, 1813*

* * *

Henry has this moment said that he likes my M.P. [*Mansfield Park*] better & better;—he is in the 3^d vol.—I beleive *now* he has changed his mind as to foreseeing the end; —he said yesterday at least, that he defied anybody to say whether H.C. [Henry Crawford] would be re- formed, or would forget Fanny in a fortnight.

　　—*from a letter to her sister, Cassandra, about their brother*

　　　Henry, March 5–8, 1814

* * *

Make everybody at Hendon admire Mansfield Park.

　　—*from a letter to her niece Anna (Austen) Lefroy,*

　　　November 22, 1814

* * *

My greatest anxiety at present is that this 4th work shd not disgrace what was good in the others. . . . whatever may be my wishes for its' success, I am very strongly haunted by the idea that to those Readers who have pre- ferred P&P. [*Pride and Prejudice*] it will appear inferior in Wit, & to those who have preferred MP. [*Mansfield Park*] very inferior in good Sense. Such as it is however, I hope

that you will do me the favour of accepting a Copy. . . . I think I may boast myself to be, with all possible Vanity, the most unlearned, & uninformed Female who ever dared to be an Authoress.

> —*from a letter to the Reverend James Stanier Clarke, domestic chaplain and librarian to the Prince Regent—later George IV—who was a fan of Austen's work, and to whom Clarke suggested she dedicate her work (a suggestion she could not refuse, as evidenced in the dedication of* Emma, *the novel of which she speaks here), December 11, 1815*

*   *   *

You are very, very kind in your hints as to the sort of Composition which might recommend me at present, & I am fully sensible that an Historical Romance, founded on the House of Saxe Cobourg, might be much more to the purpose of Profit or Popularity, than such pictures of domestic Life in Country Villages as I deal in—but I could no more write a Romance than an Epic Poem.—I could not sit seriously down to write a serious Romance under

any other motive than to save my Life, & if it were indispensable for me to keep it up & never relax into laughing at myself or at other people, I am sure I should be hung before I had finished the first Chapter.—No—I must keep to my own style & go on in my own Way; and though I may never succeed again in that, I am convinced that I should totally fail in any other.

> —*from a letter to the Reverend James Stanier Clarke, domestic chaplain and librarian to the Prince Regent—later George IV (see above)—regarding Clarke's suggestion that she try writing a historical romance, April 1, 1816*

* * *

I often wonder how *you* can find time for what you do, in addition to the care of the House;—And how good Mrs West [Jane West, a prolific author of the time] cd have written such Books & collected so many hard words, with all her family cares, is still more a matter of astonishment! Composition seems to me Impossible, with a head full of Joints of Mutton & doses of rhubarb.

> —*from a letter to her sister, Cassandra, September 8–9, 1816*

* * *

By the bye, my dear Edward, I am quite concerned for the loss your Mother mentions in her Letter; two Chapters & a half to be missing is monstrous! It is well that *I* have not been at Steventon lately, & therefore cannot be suspected of purloining them;—two strong twigs & a half towards a Nest of my own, would have been something.—I do not think however that any theft of that sort would really be very useful to me. What should I do with your strong, manly, spirited Sketches, full of Variety & Glow?—How could I possibly join them on to the little bit (two Inches wide) of Ivory on which I work with so fine a Brush, as produces little effect after much labour?

—*from a letter to her nephew James Edward Austen,*

December 16–17, 1816

* * *

Do not oblige him [Mr. Wildman, a suitor of Austen's niece, Fanny, to whom she writes] to read any more.— Have mercy on him, tell him the truth & make him an apology.—He & I should not in the least agree of course, in our ideas of Novels & Heroines;—pictures of perfection as you know make me sick & wicked—but there is some very good sense in what he says, & I particularly respect him for wishing to think well of all young Ladies; it shews an amiable & a delicate Mind.—And he deserves better treatment than to be obliged to read any more of my Works.

> —*from a letter to her niece Fanny Knight, after Fanny re-*
> *quested that Mr. Wildman read some of her aunt's books,*
> *without disclosing to him who wrote them, and passed*
> *along his opinion to her aunt, March 23–25, 1817*

* * *

BECOMING JANE

⁂

The forces of family, friendship, books, courtship, love, and other influences described throughout this book did their part in helping Jane Austen "become Jane"—that is, in shaping her into a thoroughly unique writer.

Austen's writing, like the author herself, defies attempts to neatly label it as one thing or another. It is elegant yet brazen; decorous yet bold; hilarious yet passionately earnest about the inequities of her time. Anyone who reads Austen expecting the sort of mild-mannered docility that her mob-capped image might convey is in for a surprise. Her letters brim with her own sterling brand of comedy. And the humor in her fiction, while more restrained—it was, after all,

written for the public, while her letters were decidedly not—
nonetheless often fills the most reluctant new reader with
genuine delight.

Part of Austin's genius was a gift for being able to say a lot
with a little. She was a master of one-line zingers and short
deadpan drolleries that start off sweet but break out in cleverness. So herewith, to close this compendium of her wisdom and
wit, are some of the best.

Your silence on the subject of our Ball, makes me suppose your Curiosity too great for words.

—*from a letter to her sister, Cassandra, January 24, 1809*

* * *

"It is not everyone," said Elinor, "who has your passion
for dead leaves."

—*Elinor Dashwood to her sister Marianne, in* Sense
and Sensibility

* * *

Miss Blachford is agreable enough; I do not want People to be very agreable, as it saves me the trouble of liking them a great deal.

—*from a letter to her sister, Cassandra, December 24–26, 1798*

* * *

". . . I cannot speak well enough to be unintelligible."

—*Catherine Morland, in* Northanger Abbey

* * *

You express so little anxiety about my being murdered under Ash Park Copse by Mʳˢ Hulbert's servant, that I have a great mind not to tell you whether I was or not . . .

—*from a letter to her sister, Cassandra, January 8–9, 1799*

* * *

We have been exceedingly busy ever since you went away. In the first place we have had to rejoice two or three times every day at your having such very delightful weather for the whole of your Journey . . .

    —*from a letter to her sister, Cassandra, October 25–27, 1800*

* * *

"He is such a charming man, that it is quite a pity he should be so grave and so dull."

    —*Mrs. Palmer to Elinor Dashwood, on Colonel Brandon,*
      in Sense and Sensibility

* * *

"I always deserve the best treatment, because I never put up with any other . . ."

    —*Emma Woodhouse to Mr. Knightley, in* Emma

* * *

"Nothing ever fatigues me, but doing what I do not like."

    —*Mary Crawford to Edmund Bertram, in* Mansfield Park

* * *

I will not say that your Mulberry trees are dead, but I am afraid they are not alive.

—from a letter to her sister, Cassandra, May 31, 1811

*   *   *

What is become of all the Shyness in the World? Moral as well as Natural Diseases disappear in the progress of time, & new ones take their place.—Shyness & the Sweating Sickness have given way to Confidence & Paralytic complaints.

—from a letter to her sister, Cassandra, February 8–9, 1807

*   *   *

How quick come the reasons for approving what we like!

—from Persuasion

*   *   *

How horrible it is to have so many people killed!—And what a blessing that one cares for none of them!

—from a letter to her sister, Cassandra, May 31, 1811

(on the casualty numbers reported from a recent Peninsular War battle)

✳   ✳   ✳

We plan having a steady Cook & a young, giddy House-maid, with a sedate, middle aged Man, who is to under-take the double office of Husband to the former & sweetheart to the latter. No Children of course to be al-lowed on either side.

—*from a letter to her sister, Cassandra,*
   January 3–5, 1801

✳   ✳   ✳

"One cannot always be laughing at a man without now and then stumbling on something witty."

—*Elizabeth Bennet to her sister Jane, about her "abuse" of*
   Mr. Darcy, in Pride and Prejudice

✳   ✳   ✳

". . . in a country like this . . . every man is surrounded by a neighborhood of voluntary spies . . ."

—*Henry Tilney to Catherine Morland, in*
   Northanger Abbey

* * *

It was a delightful visit;—perfect, in being much too short.

—*from* Emma

* * *

Heaven forbid that I should ever offer such encouragement to Explanations, as to give a clear one on any occasion myself.

—*from a letter to her sister, Cassandra, June 2, 1799*

* * *

By the bye, as I must leave off being young, I find many Douceurs [French for *sweetnesses*] in being a sort of Chaperon[e] for I am put on the Sofa near the Fire & can drink as much wine as I like.

—*from a letter to her sister, Cassandra, November 6–7, 1813*

* * *

. . . when the Gooseberries are ripe I shall sit upon my Bench, eat them & think of you, tho I can do that without the assistance of ripe gooseberries . . .

> —*from a letter to her niece Anna Austen (later Lefroy), probably written in mid-July,* 1814

* * *

"You have delighted us long enough."

> —*Mr. Bennet to his daughter Mary, in* Pride and Prejudice

* * *

ACKNOWLEDGMENTS

I'm grateful to the entire Hyperion team, especially: Claire McKean, for her kindness and thoughtfulness in suggesting me; Emily Gould, for hiring me for a dream job and getting me up and running; Miriam Wenger, for her intelligent and sensitive editing; Rachelle Mandik, Joseph Mills, and Vivian Gomez, for taking pains with the copyediting and proofreading process; Susan Groarke, for her flexibility and help; David Lott, for his support and encouragement; Fritz Metsch and Helene Berinsky, for creating the book's graceful interior design; Linda Prather and her team, especially Linda Lehr, for guiding it through the production process; Allison McGeehon, for her publicity savvy; and Will Schwalbe and Bob Miller, for believing that the world needed one more book about Jane Austen.

I would also like to thank Michael Luisi, Keri Putnam, and Leslie Stern, and everyone else involved with *Becoming Jane* at Miramax Films.

Special thanks go to my dear friend Cullen Stanley, of Janklow & Nesbit Associates, for her expert advice and invaluable aid in navigating the brave new world of book contracts.

I must appreciatively acknowledge the following wonderful books and Web sites, which helped immeasurably with the research for this book: *Jane Austen's Letters*, collected and edited by Deirdre Le Faye; *Jane Austen: A Family Record*, by Deirdre Le Faye; *The Friendly Jane Austen*, by Natalie Tyler; *Jane Austen for Dummies*, by Joan Klingel Ray, Ph.D.; The Republic of Pemberley Web site, www.pemberley .com; and the Jane Austen Society of North America Web site, www.jasna.org.

And, of course, my thanks to the brilliant Jane Austen, whose life and words are always an inspiration, and who makes me proud to be a maiden aunt.

Anne Newgarden is a freelance writer and editor. She has worked frequently in the field of multimedia children's content, and more recently collaborated on two pop-up books for grown-ups with author/artist Chuck Fischer, *Christmas in New York* and *Christmas Around the World*. She lives in her hometown of New York City.